CONFESSIONS
OF AN
IMAGINARY
FRIEND

a memoir by Jacques Papier
AS TOLD TO MICHELLE CUEVAS

Dial Books for Young Readers
an imprint of Penguin Young Readers Group (USA) LLC

DIAL BOOKS FOR YOUNG READERS
Published by the Penguin Group
Penguin Group (USA) LLC
375 Hudson Street
New York, New York 10014

USA/Canada/UK/Ireland/Australia/New Zealand/India/South Africa/China
penguin.com
A Penguin Random House Company

Text and interior artwork copyright © 2015 by Michelle Cuevas

Library of Congress Cataloging-in-Publication Data

Cuevas, Michelle.
Confessions of an imaginary friend / as told to Michelle Cuevas.
pages cm
Summary: "When Jacques Papier discovers he's imaginary,
he sets off on a journey to find his true home" —Provided by publisher.
ISBN 978-0-525-42755-1 (hardcover)
[1. Imaginary playmates—Fiction.] I. Title.

PZ7.C89268Co 2015
[Fic]—dc23
2014044885

Printed in the United States of America

1 3 5 7 9 10 8 6 4 2

Designed by Jasmin Rubero
Text set in Chaparral Pro

For Carly:

I couldn't imagine a better friend.

Chapter One
EVERYONE HATES JACQUES PAPIER

Yes, world, I am writing my memoir, and I have titled the first chapter simply this:

EVERYONE HATES JACQUES PAPIER

I think it captures the exact drama of my first eight years in the world rather poetically. Soon I'll move on to chapter two. This is where I'll confess that the first chapter was, in fact, the truth stretched, much like the accordion body of my wiener dog, François. The stretch would be the word *everyone*. There are three exceptions to this word. They are:

My mother.

My father.

My twin sister, Fleur.

If you are observant, you'll notice that I *did not* include François the wiener dog on this list.

Chapter Two
FRANÇOIS THE EVIL WIENER DOG

A boy and his dog are, quite possibly, the most classic of all classic duos.

Like peanut butter and jelly.

Like a left and right foot.

Like salt and pepper.

And yet.

My relationship with François more closely resembles peanut butter on a knuckle sandwich. A left foot in a bear trap. Salt and a fresh paper cut. You get the picture.

In the interest of truth, it is not entirely François' fault; the cards of life have been stacked rather steeply against him. For starters, I do not believe the person in charge of making dogs was paying attention when they attached François' stumpy legs to his banana-shaped body. Perhaps we'd all be ill-tempered if our stomachs cleaned the floor whenever we went for a walk.

The day we brought him home as a puppy, François sniffed my sister and grinned. He sniffed me and began barking—a barking that has never ceased in the eight years I've been within range of his villainous nose.

Chapter Three
PAPIER'S PUPPETS

It is true that *Papier* is the French word for paper. However, my family does not make or sell paper. No, my family is in the imagination business.

"Are there really that many people who need puppets?" Fleur asked our father. To be honest, I had often wondered the very same thing about our parents' puppet shop.

"Dear girl," our father answered. "I think the real question is, who *doesn't* need a puppet?"

"Florists," Fleur answered. "Musicians. Chefs. Newscasters . . ."

"Oh hello," Father said. "I'm a florist. They say talking to plants helps them grow, and now the puppet and I are chatting and our flowers are thriving." He spun around. "Why, look at me, the piano player, with a puppet on each hand, so now I have four arms instead of just two. I'm a chef, but instead of an oven mitt, I have a puppet to pretend with. Oh look, I'm a newscaster who once delivered the news alone, but now have a puppet for witty banter."

"Fine," Fleur said. "Lonely people without anyone to talk to need puppets. Luckily Jacques and I have each other, and we are going outside to play."

I smiled, waved to our father, and followed Fleur out the door. The bell rang as we left the cool gaze of puppets and greeted the sunshine, winking at us through afternoon clouds.

Chapter Four
NO, REALLY.
EVERYONE HATES JACQUES PAPIER.

School. Who thought of this cruel place? Perhaps it is the same person who matches together the various pieces of wiener dogs. School is a great example of a place where everyone (and I mean *everyone*) hates me. Allow me to illustrate with examples from this very week:

On Monday, our class played kickball. The captains chose players for their team one by one. When they got to me, they just went and started the game. I wasn't picked last; I wasn't picked at all.

On Tuesday, I was the only person who knew the capital of Idaho. I had my arm in the air, even waving it around like a hand puppet on the high sea. But the teacher just said, "Really? Nobody knows the answer? *Nobody?*"

On Wednesday, at lunch, a very husky boy nearly sat on me, and I had to scramble from my seat to avoid certain death.

On Thursday, I waited in line for the bus, and before I could get on, the driver shut the door. Right in my face. "Oh, COME ON!" I shouted, but the words disappeared in a cloud of exhaust. Fleur made the driver stop, got off, and walked home beside me.

And so, on Friday morning, I begged my parents to let me stay home from school. They didn't even say no. They just gave me the silent treatment.

Chapter Five
THE MAP OF US

For as long as I could remember, Fleur and I had been making The Map of Us. There were the easy to draw places: the frog pond, the field with the best fireflies, and the tree where we'd carved our initials in the trunk.

And there were the permanent fixtures in our world as well, like Puppet Shop Peak, the Fjords of François, and the Mountaintop of Mom & Dad.

But then there were the other places.

The best places.

The places that could only be found by us.

There was the stream full of tears that Fleur cried when a boy at school made fun of her teeth. The spot where we buried a time capsule. And the spot where we dug up a time capsule. And the much better place where the time capsule currently resides (for now). There was the sidewalk chalk art gallery we commission each summer. And the tree where I broke the climbing record, and also fell, but we didn't tell Mom and Dad. There was the place where the flamingoose, the bighornbear, and the ostrimpanzee roam and graze. And the knothole in the oak where I kept Fleur's smile, the one she does with her eyes instead of her mouth. There were hiding places, and finding places, and deep wells full of secrets.

Yes, like any best friends, there was a whole world that could only be seen by her and me.

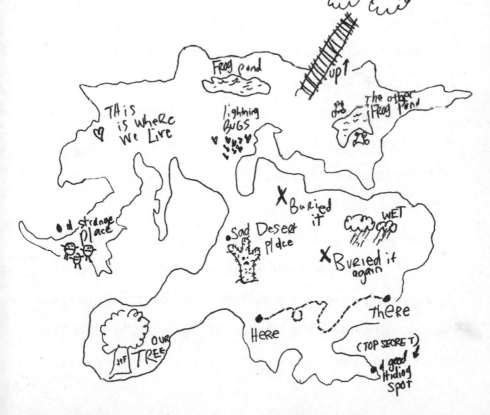

Chapter Six
MAURICE THE MAGNIFICENT

Sometimes, on Sundays, our family would go to the local kids'
museum, which was really just a bunch of bubble blowing, and
old rocks, and baby stuff like that. But that's not why we went.
We went because on Sundays you could get free popcorn and
"enjoy" the "magic" of Maurice the Magnificent.

Maurice was old. I don't mean grandparent old or even
great-grandparent old. I mean *old*. Old like the candles on his
birthday cake cost more than the cake. Old like his memories
were in black and white.

And his tricks! They were the worst. He did one where
he made a dove appear out of a phonograph. A phonograph!
This guy was at least a thousand years old. Every time we
went to his show, Fleur would lean over so I could whisper
my witty remarks.

"Maurice is so old," I whispered, "his report card was written in hieroglyphics."

Fleur covered her mouth with her hands to contain her giggles.

"He's so old," I continued, "that when he was born, the Dead Sea was just coming down with a cough."

Sadly, on that particular Sunday, neither of us noticed that Maurice the Magnificent had noticed *us* mocking his show.

"Little girl," said Maurice, pausing in front of us with a morose rabbit in his hands. "To whom are you whispering?"

"This is my brother," said Fleur. "His name is Jacques."

"Ah," said Maurice, nodding. "And what did *Jacques* say that was so very humorous?"

Fleur's cheeks turned red like her hair, and she bit her lip with embarrassment.

"Well," said Fleur. "He thinks you're . . . old. Oh, and a phony. Jacques said that none of this is real."

"I see," said Maurice. "Well, the world is full of people who will doubt."

Maurice tried to swish his cape with a flourish, hurt his back, and feebly made his way across the stage using his cane.

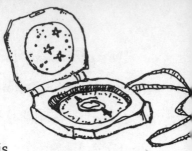

"Doubters will say that magic is only make-believe. And you know what? You don't need to say a word to prove them wrong. All you need is this."

Maurice pulled an old broken compass from his vest pocket. It looked about as old as him, and the arrow only pointed one way: directly at the person holding it.

"Come up here, little girl. You will be my assistant."

Fleur stood, and reluctantly joined Maurice on stage. I felt a twinge of guilt, and hoped he wouldn't put her in a box and stick her with swords.

"Take this," said Maurice. He handed Fleur the compass.

"I'm going to make you disappear," said Maurice. He went over to a person-sized cabinet, opened the door, and motioned for Fleur to step inside. She did, and he closed the cabinet behind her.

"Alakazam!" shouted Maurice. I couldn't help but roll my eyes.

But then, to my utter shock, Maurice opened the cabinet and Fleur was gone! An excited murmur went through the crowd.

"Now, Fleur," hollered Maurice. "If you tap your compass three times, you can come back home."

Maurice closed the cabinet, waited for three taps, and when he opened the door, *POOF!* There was Fleur.

Well, obviously the audience went wild, and old Maurice took a bow (or not; it was hard to tell since his posture was already so stooped). Fleur tried to give back the compass, but Maurice shook his head and folded Fleur's hand over it.

"The world is a mystery with a capital *M*," said Maurice. "The impossible is possible. And you, Fleur, seem like the kind of girl who knows that *real* is merely in the eye of the beholder."

Chapter Seven
FLABBERGASTED

The next day I was fiddling with the compass from the magic show, attempting to make François the wiener dog disappear, when I heard my parents enter their room. The walls in the Papier household are paper-thin, which is how I overheard the conversation that changed the course of my life.

"Do you think," I heard my mother say, "there is such a thing as *too much* imagination?"

"Perhaps," my father replied. "Maybe it was wrong to raise her around so many puppets. Maybe all those googly eyes and moving mouths confused her."

I heard my mother sigh. "And we shouldn't have played along for such a long time. The bunk beds were one thing, but setting an extra place at the table? An extra toothbrush? Buying a second set of books for school? I guess I just thought Fleur would eventually grow out of having an imaginary friend on her own."

I was shocked.

I was dumbfounded.

I was flabbergasted.

My sister, my sidekick, had an imaginary friend that she'd never told me about.

Chapter Eight
KNOWN

Oh, Fleur!

We shared everything: bunk beds, baths, banana splits. And don't even get me started on subsequent letters of the alphabet. Once we even shared—brace yourself—a piece of chewing gum. She was chewing, and I had none, and she split it in two like the King Solomon of sweets. Maybe it was yucky. Maybe it was love. And maybe it was a sticky blob of both.

And now a secret as monumental as an imaginary friend?

We were so close. Fleur could read my mind. She knew what I was thinking before I did.

"What would you like for breakfast?" our mother would ask.

And Fleur would shout back, "Jacques wants a pancake

shaped like Mozart's Symphony No. 40! In G minor!"

The weirdest part? I did want that. I *did*.

The truth is, that's all anyone wants, to be known that way, to be seen. I don't mean our hair or our clothes, I mean *seen* for who we really are. We all want to find that one person who knows the real us, all our quirks, and still understands. Have you ever had anyone see you? Really, truly, the deepest part that seems invisible to the rest of the world?

I hope you have.

I have.

I have always had Fleur.

Chapter Nine
R FOR RIDICULOUS

The next morning, I awoke slightly less depressed. My anger and confusion had been replaced with a plan. *Two can play at that game.*

I'm not talking about Go Fish or Trivial Pursuit, though I am brilliant at both. I'm talking about the imaginary friend game that Fleur was playing. I'm talking about my brilliant idea to get an imaginary friend of *my own*.

To be honest, I didn't know a ton about the topic since I'm clearly the intellectual type, more interested in pop-up vice presidential biographies and particle physics coloring books. So I went to the library to conduct my research.

"Excuse me," I said to the librarian. "Do you have any material about imaginary friends? Would that be under *I* or *F*, do you think? Maybe *R* for ridiculous! Am I right, or am I right?"

I put up my hand for a high five, but the librarian kept stacking her books, totally ignoring me. I knew what this was about.

"Look," I explained. "My dog François is a monster. *He ate those other books I took out. And I still firmly believe he should be charged the late fees, not me.*"

The librarian yawned, fixed her glasses.

"You know what, *fine*," I said, exasperated. "Old Dewey Decimal and I will just figure it out ourselves."

I searched and searched, and on a dusty shelf between a book on unicorns and a guide to the North Pole, I finally found something about imaginary friends.

imag·i·nary friend

noun

: a person whom you like and enjoy being with, but is not real

: a person who helps or supports someone, existing only in the mind or imagination

Synonyms

fanciful amigo, fantastical buddy, fictional chum, invented compadre, mythical confidant, phantom crony, pretend familiar, unreal intimate, theoretical mate [*chiefly British*], made-up musketeer

Antonyms

Existent enemy, factual foe

Habitat of Imaginary Friends

Found in trees. Sometimes also in old silent movie theaters, seaside zoos, magic shops, hat shops, time-travel shops, topiary gardens, cowboy boots, castle turrets, comet museums, dog pounds, mermaid ponds, dragon lairs, library stacks (the ones in the back), piles of leaves, piles of pancakes, the belly of a fiddle, the bell of a flower, or in the company of wild herds of typewriters.

But mostly in trees.

Migratory Patterns

Sometimes imaginary friends will have to wander, travel, or roam a great distance before encountering anyone who can see them. When they do, they usually stay for a long while.

Diet

Cloud root beer floats and moon grilled cheeses. But their favorite food is stardust.

Common Activities of Imaginary Friends

Imaginary friends spend most of their time crouched down, staring into the grass. Closer. Closer. Closer still. There. See? They are forever looking into the nooks and crannies of a thing, whatever the thing may be. Always up very early or very late, going for rides on the backs of whales who deliver the mail; waking up covered in a secret language of hums; writing about the hobbies of feathers; changing shape like a cloud; howling at the moon; being a radioactive night-light in the dark; being a life raft on an ocean of alphabet soup; being great-hearted; being selfless; believing in tall tales, doodlebugs, and doohickeys. Believing. Believing in themselves. Believing in *you*.

Chapter Ten
ME AND MY (NEW) BEST FRIEND

That imaginary friend book. What a load of nonsense!

It did, however, give me a few ideas on how to at least *pretend* I had an imaginary friend of my own.

So I didn't look too ridiculous, I only spent time with my new "friend" in private. But I always made sure Fleur was watching. First, I took out a jump rope and started flailing it wildly in the air, pretending my "friend" was holding the other end. Useless. Next my "friend" and I made a milk shake with two straws. Boy, we had some laughs, though I ended up drinking most of the shake. Turns out my new best friend doesn't care for chocolate. We played board games (I won every game), used the teeter-totter (not a lot of teeter, even less totter), and we even had a rousing round of catch (though it was mostly just me throwing). Maybe imaginary friends lack athletic prowess? I'd have to check back at the library.

Anyhow, it finally worked, because Fleur took notice, and asked what in the world I was doing.

"I'm spending some quality time bonding with my new imaginary friend. My imaginary *best* friend," I added.

"I see," said Fleur. "So what is this friend like?"

"Like?" I asked, gulping.

"Yeah, you know," said Fleur. "What does he look like? What does he like to do? What's his favorite color and song and hobbies and wishes and dreams?"

"Right, right." I nodded. "Well, uh, my friend has got sort of reddish-brownish-lightish-darkish hair. Sometimes he wears shirts. And enjoys many kinds of . . . food."

"Jacques, are you making this up?" asked Fleur.

"No!" I shouted. "He's definitely a real imaginary friend. Look, I've got a picture of him somewhere. I just need to go find it, and then we can discuss this further."

I ran out of the room, into the bedroom I shared with Fleur, and bolted the door behind me. I had bought myself some time. I sat down at my desk to get to work. I tried to think. I thought some more. Just who was my imaginary friend? But there was nothing. Nada. Blank. It was, I realized, like trying to remember details about a person I'd never even met.

Chapter Eleven
A SHORT LIST OF POTENTIAL BEST FRIENDS

But then a lightbulb went off. I had made it up, the whole thing! So I could just make up any details I wanted about this *imaginary* imaginary friend. Genius. A foolproof plan. I started to make a list of potential candidates:

My imaginary friend is a successful tax accountant who is considering opening his own office.

(Sorry. I can do better.)

My imaginary friend has a heart made out of a flower. Bees buzz around his head all day long, and he often walks around with his mouth open in the sun or the rain, hoping it will be good for his heart.

My imaginary friend is a giant. He juggles the earth, along with other planets, and that's what makes them spin. He doesn't drop the earth often, but when he does, ceramic tea-cups from England fall off the globe, or the spots fall off the leopards in Africa.

My imaginary friend's father was a big fish who lived in the sea, and his mother was a mermaid and her scales were colored green.

My imaginary friend looks like a potato and has the same personality.

Chapter Twelve
THE GREAT DRAGON HERRING

Once I'd finally decided on the details of my imaginary friend, I went and found Fleur.

"Behold!"

I held up the extremely realistic drawing I had made all by myself.

"I present . . . the Great Dragon Herring!"

"Wow," said Fleur. "That's amazing."

"I know," I said proudly.

Fleur paused. "So . . . what is it?"

"A Great Dragon Herring, of course," I replied.

"I get it. It's part dragon," said Fleur.

"And part fish," I said, finishing the thought.

"What does it eat?" asked Fleur.

"It eats cloud root beer floats and moon grilled cheeses and its favorite food is stardust," I replied.

"Well, Dad said we're having meat loaf for dinner," said Fleur.

I turned around and pretended to whisper, in deep conversation with a dragon who wasn't actually there.

"Yeah," I said finally. "It'll eat meat loaf too."

We made our way to the kitchen, where our parents were making dinner. There were four places set at the table, as usual.

"We need to set a fifth place at the table," said Fleur.

"For whom?" asked our mother.

"Jacques has a new imaginary friend," explained Fleur. "It's part dragon and part fish, but willing to try your meat loaf."

"How flattering," said our mother. I sensed a hint of sarcasm in her voice.

Our father stopped stirring a pan on the stove. Our mother sat down, closed her eyes, and rubbed her temple like she was having another one of her migraines.

"So now Jacques has his own imaginary friend?" asked our mother. "Don't you think that's a bit . . . excessive?"

"Not really," said Fleur, fetching an extra plate and fork. "Aren't you always saying to expand our imaginations?"

At this, our mother pointed a blaming finger at our father. He was, in fact, always saying corny things like that.

And so, trapped by Fleur's logic, our parents had to squeeze around the table with Fleur, a giant imaginary Dragon Herring, and yours truly. I'll admit it was a bit cramped.

After dinner, we went to a movie and Fleur insisted my parents buy an extra ticket for my imaginary friend. That's when Dad realized he'd already seen the movie, so we got ice-cream cones instead—the whole family, including the Dragon Herring, who, it turned out, had a taste for rocky road. And late that night, when Fleur had a nightmare, we all climbed into our parents' bed for protection. The Dragon Herring, however, took up too much room, and our father was pushed out of the bed and flopped to the floor. Which is when he started screaming.

"THAT'S IT! I've had it! This is just . . . just . . . *too much imagination!*" he yelled. He stood in his robe, his hair on end like a madman. "It's just too many layers," he continued. "A girl having an imaginary friend is one thing. But an imaginary friend who has *his own imaginary friend*? No, no, it's too much. It's like a nesting doll of imagination! It's like a painting of a painting! It's like the wind catching a chill from the wind, or a wave taking a dip in the ocean. It's like reading a novel that merely describes another novel. It's like music tapping its foot to a tune and saying 'Oh! I love this song!'"

Perhaps we had finally pushed our father too far.

But I couldn't think about that. All I could think about was what he'd said first.

An imaginary friend who has his own imaginary friend.

I had no idea what he meant by that, but was starting to get an uneasy feeling in the pit of my stomach.

Chapter Thirteen
THE ROLLER–SKATING COWGIRL

The sun was setting as I sipped the last drops from the bottom of my juice box. I finished, crumpled the box, and tossed it in the pile behind the swing set with the rest.

I sat without swinging. My head hung heavy with troubles and sugar, like a cowboy's after a long night riding the range.

"How many of those you had, pardner?"

I looked up to see a girl my age dressed in cowgirl gear. Instead of boots she wore roller skates with spurs on the sides.

"What's it to you?" I grumbled.

"This seat taken?" she asked, motioning to the other swing. "Would you like to talk about whatever's giving you the blues, buckaroo?"

"No," I replied. "I most certainly do not want to talk about my sister. I don't want to chat about how she has an imaginary friend that she never even told me existed. And I definitely don't want to discuss how they're probably off having a tea party or getting matching tattoos as we speak."

"Ah," said the skating cowgirl. "Imaginary problems. Those are the worst."

"Sure," I said, stabbing a plastic straw into the opening of another juice box. "Go ahead. Mock my pain."

"I'm not," said the girl. "See that gal over there? The one in the cowboy hat, spinning on the merry-go-round?"

I looked over and saw the girl. The merry-go-round slowed to a stop, the gears clinking like the last notes of a music box.

"Well, the thing is . . . the truth of the matter, if you must know, is that . . ."

And then she said the words that changed everything, that etched in my heart like carvings on the trunk of a tree:

"I am her imaginary friend."

Chapter Fourteen
HOWL, CRICKET, SING

The cowgirl's words leaped around my head, bouncing like crickets in a field when a person walked too close.

"You're *imaginary*?" I asked.

"Yes, very much so," replied the girl.

"Baloney," I replied.

"Believe me or don't. Doesn't matter to me," said the girl.

I narrowed my eyes.

"Suppose," I said, "we pretend for a moment that I believe you. Fine. You're an imaginary roller-skating cowgirl. But then, the question remains—why in the world can *I* see you?"

The girl wheeled her skates back and forth below the swing for a moment, deep in thought. The leaves on the trees splashed us in light and shadow.

"How do I put this delicately?" she said. "You've heard

dogs howling before, right? And crickets cricketing? And birds singing?"

"Of course."

"Well, you and I have no idea what the crickets or the dogs or the birds are saying to one another. However, two little birds could duet all day, and two crickets can understand each other's chirps. And why is that?"

"Because they're the same," I replied.

"The same! Exactly!"

I stared at the girl in the skates. I shook my head.

"Oh dear." She sighed. "You really, truly don't know, do you?"

"Know *what*?" I asked. "That you're a crazy person? Yes, I do know that."

"Let me ask you," said the cowgirl. "Do you have to just take whatever desk is empty at school? Avoid cars? Bikes? Does anyone other than your sister ever talk to you? Do you sometimes feel like you're, I don't know, *invisible*?"

"Everyone feels like that sometimes," I said, my voice becoming small. "Right . . . ?"

And with that, I rose from my swing and hurried away from the park.

Chapter Fifteen
DANCING DUST

I spent the next day moping on my top bunk. I looked around the room. The sun was rising, and pillars of light streamed inside. The beams, filled with dancing dust, attached the two windows to the floor. For some reason, the idea struck me that maybe these were the real things that kept our house from falling down. Not the beams or the nails, but something else. Something that couldn't be seen with the eyes, but was there underneath everything.

I stayed there thinking until day turned to night. I looked out at the deep blue sky and the dots of starlight. I stayed there until Fleur went to bed in her bottom bunk.

"Fleur, what do you think stars are made from?"

"Dunno," she said, starting to doze.

Maybe we're made of the same things as stars, and stars

are made of the same stuff as us. Made from all the things that are lost, and all the things that don't belong.

Our mother came to tuck us in. She turned on the night-light and came over to the bunk beds.

"Good night," she said, brushing Fleur's hair back from her face. "Sleep tight, don't let the bedbugs bite."

"Now say it to Jacques," said Fleur.

"Good night, Jacques. Sleep tight."

"And the bugs," protested Fleur.

"Right." Our mother smiled. "Listen up, bedbugs. No biting Jacques."

Then she pulled the covers tight around Fleur's chin. She tucked in the edges and kissed her forehead.

"I love you, Fleur."

Fleur closed her eyes. "Now say it to Jacques."

"I love you, Jacques," she said, then got up and walked out, leaving a thin frame of light glowing around the closed door.

Chapter Sixteen
EVERYONE (STILL) HATES JACQUES PAPIER

I decided to experiment.

On Monday I stood in the middle of the kickball field during a game, among the smell of long grass and the taste of gnats. I sang—no joke—one hundred and seventy-four verses of "John Jacob Jingleheimer Schmidt." Nobody noticed. Not even the gnats.

On Tuesday I tap-danced on my teacher's desk during a geography lesson. She just kept teaching about fjords. Fjords!

On Wednesday I bet the cafeteria crowd I could eat an entire tray full of individual cups of butterscotch pudding for lunch. "Hey," I hollered. "I bet I can eat the most butterscotch pudding!" Nobody took the challenge. I won by default.

On Thursday, I stood outside the dining room and

watched my family eat dinner. Dad put out a plate of chicken surprise for me and everything. He said (for Fleur's benefit, I assume), "Now Jacques, eat up. It's your favorite."

"Jacques isn't even *there*," said Fleur.

"Of course he is," clucked our mother. "He's sitting right there, like always. Isn't he?"

And so, by Friday, I had Jingleheimer-induced laryngitis, bug bites, a stomachache, and a plethora of useless information about fjords. I began to wonder: Do I even like chicken surprise? *Do* I?

That's when I, Jacques Papier, normally calm, collected, and in need of no assistance, started to officially panic.

EDITORIAL NOTE:
In light of recent developments, I have decided to temporarily retitle that last chapter. Here is the revision. Thank you for understanding.

~~Chapter Sixteen~~
~~EVERYONE (STILL) HATES JACQUES PAPIER~~

Chapter Sixteen
MAYBE NO ONE HATES JACQUES PAPIER
(BECAUSE MAYBE NO ONE IS AWARE HE EXISTS)

Chapter Seventeen
THE TIDE'S ROLLING IN

"Y'all came back again, I see." It was the cowgirl in skates. She once again sat beside me on the swings in the park.

"I have no desire to speak to you. If it weren't for you," I explained, "I would have gone on in blissful ignorance. Now I'm questioning everything. I don't know up from down! My life is more dismal than a wiener dog's!"

I knew I was being a tad dramatic, but it felt good to have someone to blame.

"So you understand now?" asked the cowgirl. "What you are?"

"But I have a bed," I protested. "I have a place at the table. I have a seat in the car."

The girl just nodded, allowing the thoughts to tumble out of me like fireflies from a jar, all lit up and glowing mad.

"I have pictures I drew on the fridge. Though, I suppose

Fleur always helped with those. Wait! Yes. Every year I have a birthday party. Of course, we are twins, so it's always Fleur's party as well. And we do always share a cake . . ."

That's when I had to place my head between my legs. "I'm having a heart attack!" I yelled between wheezing breaths. "Call a hospital! Call the police! Get me a defibrillator!"

"Don't get your spurs in a tangle," said the cowgirl in an effort to calm me. She rubbed my back. "Just breathe. It's really not so bad, you know."

"Not so bad?" I asked, raising my red face to hers. "Yesterday I thought I was a *boy*. Now I'm, what? Ethereal? Intangible? *Invisible?*"

"The truth is," she replied, "you're only as invisible as you feel, imaginary or not."

"Well," I said, my voice small, "I feel like air. I feel like wind. I feel like I'm made of sand, and the tide's rolling in."

Chapter Eighteen
IN WHICH I, JACQUES PAPIER, SUFFER AN EXISTENTIAL CRISIS

I became very blue.

Okay, I'll be honest, that's an understatement. I was way beyond blue. I moved into shades of navy and indigo and midnight. I got so low, my insides must have turned the color of deep space, of burned campfire, of the dark up a dragon's nose in a dungeon.

I took to my bed. I didn't move. I didn't bathe. I didn't even bother to eat, or drink, or join the family for origami craft night. What was the point? Imaginary people can only fold imaginary paper swans.

Fleur was, of course, concerned.

"I don't care what anybody thinks," said Fleur. "You're real to me."

"Okay, fine," I said. "But what am I made of, Fleur? Not anything you can touch. Not anything you can see."

"There are lots of real things you can't touch or see," replied Fleur. "There's music, and wishes, and gravity. There's electricity! And feelings. And silence."

"Oh!" I said. "How wonderful. Happy day, everything is solved. I mean, sure, you're made of the same stuff as flowers and the moon and dinosaurs. And I'm the same as *gravity*? Perfect. Stupendous. What was I worried about?"

Fleur stared at me, biting her lower lip the way she did when she was scared, or confused, or about to cry.

"We should do something today to cheer you up," she said

softly. "We could work on your bucket list."

She went over to the desk, opened a drawer, and took out my list.

"Like this one," she said, pointing to the paper. "We could put a trained ninja scorpion in François' food bowl."

I groaned and put a blanket over my head in reply.

"Or," she said, continuing to read, "we could put François' dog house in a tree while he's sleeping and see how confused he is when he wakes up. Or number three seems fun: We could dress François as a baby and leave him on the steps of an orphanage. Though I'm not sure where to find lengthy enough baby clothes . . ."

"Fleur!" I shouted. "Just forget it, okay? Nothing's going to help. I'd tell you my heart is broken, and that it's unfixable, but I can't."

"Why not?" asked Fleur.

"Because," I said, "I'm not so sure imaginary things even have hearts."

Chapter Nineteen
THE POTS, THE PANS, AND OUR WHOLE SILLY LIVES

I tried to picture how my imaginary heart would break, if I did in fact have one. Would it look like a slow leak in a snow globe, or like a popped balloon? Like a finish line ribbon the day after a race, or the hands of a broken clock that can no longer tell time? Like a snapped banjo string, or a key that breaks in a lock?

To get away from my own thoughts, I spied on Fleur and our parents in the kitchen. Fleur, it seemed, was dealing with some distressing issues as well. Her voice sounded odd, like she was an acrobat balancing words on her nose, worried they would crash to the ground at any moment and shatter.

"If Jacques is imaginary," said Fleur, "but he never knew, and now he does, then maybe *I'm* imaginary too. Or you,

Mom. Or Dad. Or all of us. The pots, the pans, the ceiling, the sky, the weather, the grass, our whole silly lives!"

Fleur pointed to François the wiener dog.

"Is that dog an imaginary dog?"

She got down on all fours and pressed her nose to François'.

"Are you real?" Fleur shouted at François. "Well, *are you?* Answer me!"

Fleur seemed to be going insane. And over nothing. I mean, who in their right mind would imagine something as unpleasant as a wiener dog?

That night our parents took us to a musical, a funny one, which they thought might cheer us up. But then, right in the middle of a rather silly can-can number involving exotic animals, Fleur got out of her seat, walked up the aisle, and climbed onto the stage.

"Is that our daughter?" gasped our mother. "What in the world is she doing?"

"How should I know?" whispered our father.

Fleur planted herself like a tree in the center of the stage, legs wide, arms crossed. Luckily, the actors playing hippos and monkeys and alligators were true professionals, and knew that the show must go on. So they ignored Fleur, and simply danced around her.

"You see," said Fleur in the car on the way home. "I am imaginary. I walked right onstage, and nobody even noticed."

Our mother popped two pills for her headache. "No more of this, Fleur," she said sternly.

Fleur agreed. But the very next day our father had to leave work to respond to a call from the police. While I was watching the chameleons camouflage themselves in the reptile house, Fleur had climbed into the gorilla pit across the zoo.

"Was she hurt?" asked our panicked parents when they arrived at the zoo offices. They found Fleur there, wrapped in a blanket and sipping hot cocoa.

"Hurt?" shouted Fleur. "The gorilla didn't even notice me! Because I'm clearly invisible." She stomped out of the office and toward the car.

"Lucky kid," said the zookeeper, shaking his head and handing my parents some paperwork to sign. "She climbed into the cage of Penelope, the blind and deaf gorilla."

Chapter Twenty
THE MERMAID AND THE HORSE

"What are these puppets doing here at the house?" asked
Fleur. "Shouldn't they be at the shop?"

"Well," said our father, his arms full of dolls and strings,
"our parenting book said sometimes it's helpful to use toys
for us to talk to one another."

"Talk about what?" asked Fleur.

"Oh, anything," replied our father. "School, hobbies,
obsessive and irrational fears that you or your loved ones are
imaginary. Stuff like that."

Our mother rolled her eyes. Clearly this had been our
father's idea. We watched as he put a horse puppet on his
hand and gave Fleur a puppet dressed like a mermaid.

"Hello," said our father in his best horse voice. "How are
you? How are you feeling today?"

Fleur begrudgingly put the mermaid onto her hand.

"I feel good. Today I swam through a shipwreck where I met a fish living in a teapot. I made a wish on a starfish. I used some squid ink to write a letter."

"Uh, no," said our father, back to his father voice. "You're not pretending to *be* the mermaid. You're you. Fleur. The puppet is just . . . uh . . . hold on."

Our father took off the horse puppet and began flipping through his parenting book, mumbling and skimming dog-eared pages.

"Oh, for goodness' sake," said our mother.

She knelt down to eye level with Fleur. "Sweetie, we made you an appointment with a psychiatrist. There's no exam or shots or anything like that. You just talk. And we'll be right there too."

Fleur considered this.

"Can Jacques come?"

Our mother spoke through gritted teeth. "Of course. I'm sure the therapist would love to meet him."

"Can he bring his imaginary friend?" asked Fleur. "The Great Dragon Herring?"

Our mother closed her eyes. "Sure. Fine. Whatever. I'm just going to lie down."

"Great," said Fleur. "But for the record, this all seems like a waste of time. I mean, we've seen pretty convincing evidence that *I'm* imaginary. Why, I bet . . ."

Fleur used her mermaid hand to pick up a frying pan.

"I bet if this mermaid hit me over the head with this frying pan," she continued, "I wouldn't even feel it. Ready?"

Our father was absorbed in his parenting book and our mother's eyes were closed.

"One," said Fleur. "Two . . . three . . ."

Chapter Twenty-one
MR. PITIFUL

And that is how we ended up in the emergency room, followed the next day by a trip for the whole family—myself included—to a psychiatrist's office.

Dr. Stéphane specialized in children and, it seemed, especially specialized in children with imaginary friends. I made a mental note to ask to see his credentials. But I didn't get a chance because when Fleur's name was called, the doctor had the nerve to ask me to stay outside in the waiting room.

After they had gone, a bespectacled, spaghetti-armed superhero looked me over.

"First time?" he asked. He sat beside a nervous, small boy who clutched the hero's cape like a security blanket. "I'm Mr. Pitiful, mediocre, not-quite-super-enough-to-be-a-superhero hero. I'm the imaginary friend of Arnold, my sidekick."

Mr. Pitiful pointed to the boy beside him. The boy, in turn, mumbled something unintelligible.

"Arnold was wondering," said Mr. Pitiful, "why the girl you're with is here."

"Actually," I replied, "she's my sister. And we're here because she thinks she's imaginary too." I paused, and added quickly, "Also, she recently went onstage during a musical, jumped into a gorilla cage, and hit herself over the head with a frying pan."

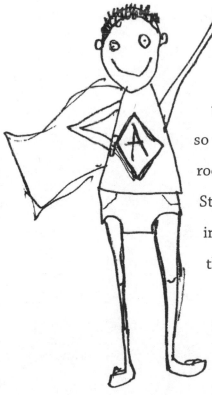

"I understand," said Mr. Pitiful knowingly. "We started coming when Arnold thought he wasn't brave enough, so he tried to fly off the garage roof with me. As the brilliant Dr. Stéphane says: 'Sometimes imaginary troubles are harder to bear than actual ones.'"

I looked around at the other imaginary friends in the waiting room. These were the only ones I'd ever seen other than the roller-skating cowgirl. There was a large, furry blob of a creature reading a magazine with a small girl, a ninja in the corner practicing moves with a boy, and there was—at least, I was pretty sure there was—an imaginary friend shaped like a red sock.

He sat at a distance from everyone else with a dirty boy and two very tidy, anxious-looking parents.

"Psssst," I said, leaning toward the sock, who, I realized, smelled like old cats and ogre feet. Like slug slime and minnow breath.

"Are you . . . an imaginary sock?" I asked.

"No, kid," replied the sock, rolling his eyes. "I'm a meatball sandwich."

"What are you here for?" I asked.

The stinky sock seemed surprised. "You really wanna hear my story?"

"Yes," I said. "Of course."

And so, from that pungent seat, the stinky sock told me his brief but odiferous tale.

Chapter Twenty-two
STINKY SOCK'S BRIEF BUT ODIFEROUS TALE

"I am," said the sock proudly, "the imaginary friend to the world's messiest little boy. And he, unfortunately, is the child of the world's tidiest parents.

"You've never seen anything like it. His mother doesn't just dust dust bunnies. She *hunts* them. She *kills* them. And his father? He only allows food to be served that matches the family wardrobe. Green on Mondays. Red on Wednesdays. And, least popular of all, blechy brown Sundays. The only songs allowed are marches—no be-bopping to offbeat tunes, or messy drum solo surprises. The boy, my friend, is constantly making messes, and constantly being yelled at. Why, sometimes I think that's why we get along so well.

"Once we met," continued the sock, "there was no stopping

us. We'd make disgusting, stinky, garbage-filled messes, the likes of which you've never seen— messes under the dinner table, buried in the clean laundry, even at the bottom of his mother's purse. 'What is that *smell*!?' they would shout over and over. 'It smells like whale belches and mustache crumbs. Like stale dreams and moldy milk stew. It smells . . . like *dirty socks*!' And the boy and I would just laugh and laugh. For I may be invisible to the eye, but the messes we made were certainly noticeable to any nose.

"Alas, in the end, it was our stinky shenanigans that separated me from the little boy. His parents, tidy as they were, just couldn't live in a house with the residue of such smells. So they packed up their bags, and their boy, and they drove away so fast I was left behind. There I was, standing in the stinky house, a condemned sign nailed to the door. And my boy? He waved back, sadly, from the rear window of the glossiest, most perfectly polished car in the entire world.

"They thought I was gone, those parents, and they were overjoyed. You could have eaten sticky buns off the floors of that new house and not picked up a speck. But then, one day, I arrived. I made it. It took me months, but I was *back*, stinkier than ever from the road. And that, you see, is how we all ended up here at the psychiatrist: just a boy, his imaginary sock, and two obsessively hygienic parents at their wits' end."

Chapter Twenty-three
AN INVITATION

When I went to the shelf to get a magazine, I realized I could hear Fleur's therapy session through the door. Was it wrong of me to listen? Yes. It was both unethical and invasive. It was like reading someone's diary, or pawing through their dirty laundry, or eating their trash (a boundary frequently violated by François). But did I press my ear to the door and listen anyhow?

You bet I did.

"Fleur, why don't you describe Jacques?" It was the voice of the (alleged) medical professional, Dr. Stéphane.

"Where to start?" replied Fleur. "He can draw all the kinds of dragons. He can type almost twelve words per minute. He knows the names of all the presidential pets. He's never had the hiccups. He taught me how to lie on the lawn, press my nose into the grass, and look around. It's like looking at a whole other planet full of alien bugs and weird smells when you do that." Fleur paused. "And also, he doesn't really have any other friends besides me. I guess that must be hard on him."

"Is that why you wished to be imaginary also?" asked Dr. Stéphane. "So Jacques wouldn't feel so alone?"

I took my ear away from the door. I was pretty sure I already knew the answer to that question.

"Hey, new guy," said Mr. Pitiful. "You should come to our group."

"What kind of group?" I asked.

"It's called Imaginaries Anonymous," replied Mr. Pitiful.

"Imaginaries Anonymous," I repeated. "Isn't that a pretty redundant name?"

"It's a support group," explained Stinky Sock. "For troubled imaginary friends. Sometimes it's nice to be surrounded by things like yourself."

I'd never really been around things like me—things that couldn't be seen or heard, not in the traditional way. Maybe they could understand. Hey, even dead leaves curl together under the blankets of snow in the winter. Even the dark crowds together at daybreak in the corners and backs of drawers.

"I'm in," I said. "Where do we meet?"

Chapter Twenty-four
IMAGINARIES ANONYMOUS

"I'm only as invisible as I feel, imaginary or not."

I was sitting in a pink playhouse in a backyard, holding hands with an array of group members, and repeating the mantra of Imaginaries Anonymous.

"Who would like to start the share?" asked Stinky Sock.

A giant imaginary raised his hand sheepishly.

"Hi. My name is The Everything. I've been imaginary for about two years now."

"Hi, Everything," said the group in unison.

The Everything was just as he said—made up of buttons and old shoes, a kite, a banana peel, and just about everything else.

"I realized I was imaginary last year," continued The

Everything. "It was when I was being blamed for shaving the family cat. My best friend blamed me, which was okay by me since I couldn't get grounded like he could. But then his parents got real mad, and said that it wasn't my fault Mr. Tickles was nude, because I was imaginary and imaginary things can't shave cats."

"And how did that make you feel?" asked Stinky Sock.

"Bad," said The Everything. "And sad. Like I'm not in control of my own fate. It's not like I *want* to shave cats. But I'd still like the option, ya know?"

Everyone nodded with understanding. There were other imaginaries at the meeting—a fat orange bird with the head of a hippo, and a purple furry monster with teeny-tiny wings on its back. There was also a shadowy figure who hid in the corner, plus Mr. Pitiful and, to my delight, the roller-skating cowgirl.

"So we meet again, pardner," said the cowgirl, smiling. "I see you've finally skated on round to the truth, no defibrillator necessary."

The cowgirl turned toward the group.

"My name is the Roller-Skating Cowgirl, and I've been imaginary for as long as I can remember. I guess lately I've been thinking a lot about, well . . . the end."

A murmur went through the crowd.

"She's growing up," continued the cowgirl. "The little girl I live with. We used to pretend to skate all around the world together. We were good too. We'd skate through fields of yellow flowers and pick bouquets without having to stop. We'd skate up volcanoes, and down to the bottom of the ocean, where we'd roll through miles of canyons and algae forests, and come up skating on the back of a whale. But then, things changed. We stopped skating so much, and then lately not at all. Yesterday, her mother was donating a bunch of old toys and said, 'Dear, do you need these skates? They're getting pretty rusty.' And my little buckaroo said, 'No, I'm too big for skates.' She threw them away! And *poof*, just like that, our trip around the world was over."

Chapter Twenty-five
THE LIGHT OF THE MOON

"As some of you probably noticed," said Stinky Sock, "we have a new member of our group. His name is Jacques Papier. Jacques, would you like to tell us why you're here?"

"Well," I said, "I'm not actually here. That's why I'm . . . here."

"Whoa," said The Everything. "Deep."

"I guess the thing is," I began, "I'm kind of wondering, what's the point of me at all? I mean, I've lived my whole eight years thinking that I was a real person. And then I learned the truth. And now that I've thought about it, I realize that I don't want to be someone's imaginary brother. I think I want to be real."

The Everything reached over and patted my hand.

"Just because you're not 'real' doesn't mean you're not

real." The Everything pointed to his own giant chest, where a heart would be if he had one. In his case, he was pointing to an old milk carton.

"I think it's like the earth and the moon," I explained. "The light of the moon is an illusion. It's actually just reflecting light from the sun, bouncing it back  like a mirror. We're like that moon, and without the people who imagined us, it's all darkness. Is that what you want? Because I don't. I want more. I want to be free."

Chapter Twenty-six
OOGLY BOOGLY

After the meeting, I stood alone eating a stale cookie, drinking a cup of grape juice, and trying to digest what I'd heard and, perhaps even more so, what I myself had said. I was so absorbed in thought, I hardly noticed when a dark storm cloud passed over and left me shrouded in shadow.

"Greetings," said a voice like a rusty bicycle.

I looked up. I tried to swallow my cookie, but my throat had become terribly dry. I coughed, crumbs scattering onto the shadowy figure in front of me. He brushed them away with no small amount of disdain.

"I'm the Oogly Boogly," he said. The rusty bicycle voice, I noted, also had a British accent.

The Oogly Boogly was hard to describe. Not because I lack the vocabulary, but because he wasn't any one thing.

His body actually came and went into focus like he was made of smoke—one minute he had warts like rotten crab apples, and then he changed and had spiders crawling from his ears. It looked as if his nose hairs were home to slugs, slime, and snails, but then he changed again, and had howling eyes, crow-beak teeth, and a beard of thunderclouds below.

"What are you?" I asked. "Are you really someone's imaginary friend?" I found it hard to believe that anyone would imagine him on purpose. Compared to this guy, François the evil wiener dog looked about as intimidating as a bowl of cold soup.

"Oh, you know me," said the Oogly Boogly, moving his face a bit too close for comfort. "I'm the Monster in the Closet. Some call me the Creature Under the Bed. Other times, I become the Thing That Goes Bump in the Night. I'm really not a bad bloke, honest. I'm just imagined that way."

"Did you say *bloke*?" I asked.

"Why," he said, a bit nervous. "Isn't that the right word?"

All of a sudden, his voice was sounding different.

"Are you doing a *fake* British accent?" I asked.

"Maybe . . ." replied the Oogly Boogly. "I thought it would be scarier."

"I guess it's kind of scary," I said. "Scary how *bad* it is."

The Oogly Boogly and I stood and stared at each other in silence for a moment.

"Oh, look at the time," I said. "Well, pleasure talking, must be going, got a Bundt cake baking in the oven back home . . ."

The Oogly Boogly put out a murky foot to stop me.

"It sounded in the meeting like you're looking for something," he said. "A thing that the sweet, naive members of this group just can't offer you."

"And you can?" I asked.

"I can," he said, tapping my nose, causing a chill down my spine. "I know how to be free. I know how to become real. I'll tell you, but it comes at a price."

"I don't really have any money," I explained. "Or an allowance or a job . . ."

"What about that?" he asked, pointing to my pocket.

I reached inside and took out the compass that had been given to Fleur by Maurice the Magnificent.

Since it was broken anyhow, I handed him the useless compass.

Sure, I thought. Whatever, weirdo, just tell me before I die of the creeps.

So the Oogly Boogly did just that. He leaned in and whispered his cobweb-covered secrets into my ear.

Chapter Twenty-seven
A MAP OF ME

That evening, when Fleur finally found me, I was on the floor of our bedroom, crayons all over my lap like oversized sprinkles on a Jacques Papier sundae.

"Whatcha drawing?" she asked.

Spread across the floor was the Map of Us we'd been constructing. I had, however, added an island off the coast. It wasn't too big, but not too small, and had a certain air of brilliance about it.

"I've decided," I said, "that I need my own island. An Island of I, if you will. An Island of Me."

"But there's nothing on it," said Fleur.

On that point, she was right.

"Well, I don't know what's there yet," I explained. "I can make out a few shadowy things, but nothing specific. That's the best part about my island. Anything is possible there. Heck, maybe there are Dragon Herrings. Maybe there's stardust, and cloud root beer floats, and meat loaf for us to eat."

"How are you going to get there?" asked Fleur. "It's hard to get to an island. You need a boat, or a plane, or a submarine."

"There's a way," I said. "The Oogly Boogly told me how to be free."

Fleur pouted. "I don't even know who that is," she said. "And how are you not free?"

It was, I knew, a very philosophical question—one I'd thought about long and hard.

"Think of it this way," I said. "If I'm a genie, then you are the lamp. I am the barnacle to your whale, the character to your novel, the tides pulled by your moon. I'm your puppet. I am nothing more than a specimen in the Museum of Fleur's Imagination."

"Well, I don't think of you that way," said Fleur.

"I know," I said. "Because you're the best sister ever. But I'm not the best brother. I'm just a part of you. And all I know is that I see people at the movies or at the grocery store, and I think about how all of them have their own epic story that swirls around them, full of their own dreams, and hopes, and fears, and allergies, and weird phobias. I don't have any of that."

"Oh," said Fleur. "Do you want me to imagine you differently?"

"Actually," I said softly, "the Oogly Boogly gave me the scissors, and I want you to cut my strings. I want to be set free."

"But how?" she asked.

And then, I shared the Oogly Boogly's secret with Fleur.

Chapter Twenty-eight
A LIST OF WHAT I, JACQUES PAPIER, PLANNED TO DO WITH MY FREEDOM

Soon I would navigate the seas like a pirate, my ship a sea turtle with sails, my crew comprised of swordfish and marlins.

I would join the circus, and eat cotton candy for every meal. I'd teach the lion to jump through a ring of fire, and then I'd jump through myself, scorching my freckles a deeper orange red.

I would learn Greek, and Latin, and at least three languages I would invent myself.

I would fly around the world, and build castles

out of snow with working lights inside that turn on at night and guide everyone home.

I would become a famed pastry chef, specializing in mud pies, dandelion donuts, and cakes decorated with moss.

I would see people, even when they were invisible.

I would walk around the world.

And my hair would grow long.

And birds would nest in my beard.

And I would get scars.

And smile wrinkles around my eyes.

I would have birthdays.

And get older.

And celebrate seasons.

I would finally be alive with a capital A.

Chapter Twenty-nine
BOOT-SCOOTIN' BUCKAROO

When I found Cowgirl she was in her stocking feet near the park. She kneeled over, revved one roller skate in each hand on the sidewalk like toy cars, and then pushed them forward in a sad, slanted road race.

"Weeeeeee . . ." she said with zero enthusiasm. "Giddy-up."

"Hey. Where's your kid?" I asked.

"Oh," said Cowgirl with a blush and a shrug. "She had some party-sleepover-cool-kids-truth-or-dare thing. I stayed here. No big deal."

"Anyhoo," I said in reply, "let me tell you what's been going on with *me*. I've been doing a lot of soul searching, thinking things like *Who is Jacques Papier? What is Jacques Papier? What does Jacques Papier want? What does Jacques Papier need? What will make Jacques Papier happy?*"

"Wow," said Cowgirl.

"I know," I replied. "Deep stuff, right?"

"I meant, 'Wow, there sure is a lot of *Jacques Papier* in those questions,'" she replied.

"Right," I said, "well, I've made a decision. I'm leaving to find out the answers to those questions."

"Wait," said Cowgirl, "before you boot-scoot away, buckaroo, there's something important you need to know—"

"Silence!" I said forcefully, putting my hand up to her. "I don't want to hear any of your reasons for staying. I just came to say good-bye. And thanks. You told me the truth when nobody else would."

"Hold on . . . wait a second . . ." said Cowgirl.

But her words didn't reach me. Like tumbleweed moving on, I was already gone.

Chapter Thirty
TINY THINGS

After much thinking about the Oogly Boogly's secret, Fleur came and found me reading a book beneath the porch light. I knew by her face that she'd nearly made her decision.

"If I do it," she asked, "what will happen? Will you disappear, or be different, or something even worse?"

"I'm not sure," I said. It was the truth. I liked the words *free* and *real*, but they didn't exactly tell the full story of what was to come.

"Maybe," I said, "I'll be able to do whatever I want whenever I want, just like you."

"I don't get to do whatever I want," said Fleur. "Like right now. I don't want things to change. But they have. They will. What if you forget all about me? What if you never come back?"

"That won't happen," I said. "I'll never forget you. I'll come back."

I pointed to her chest.

"You know what's in there? A little tree the size of a twig with a *J* and an *F* carved in the side."

"What do you mean?" said Fleur. "Like a medical condition?"

I laughed. "I mean metaphorically speaking. And there are also two little bunk beds made of matchsticks and twine. And a flea-sized François. And all our puppets, and pancake breakfasts, and hiding places, and secrets, and snores."

"I don't snore," said Fleur. But she still smiled. She'd always liked tiny, beautiful things like dollhouse furniture, or mouse houses, or small favors when nobody was looking. I liked the idea as well, though I wasn't quite sure it was true. The Oogly Boogly hadn't told me what would happen next; he had only told me how to be free. Life after that looked like a locked door leading to a part of the map that I had never explored.

"I'm ready," I told Fleur, squeezing her hand, closing my eyes.

She smiled a sad smile.

She closed her eyes too.

And then, Fleur did the tiny, beautiful thing of imagining with all her might that I was free.

Chapter Thirty-one
SAILING AWAY

Once upon a time there was a boy who didn't really exist. He lived in a house where anything was possible and everywhere was waiting to be discovered. A hedgerow was a castle. A stick a sword. Dandelion seeds the dust needed for magic.

Once there was a boy, and he had a sister, and they were best friends. They made up endless maps together—he would be captain of the forest and she would be navigator. They made up songs about birds flying backward, about notes lost in bottles, about caterpillars pining to be butterflies. In the glowing late summer light, they carved two initials, one J and one F, into the side of a tree. They gathered magic in their small hands, tumbled home each evening, and fell asleep with leaves of grass in their hair.

The boy wished to be something else, but what, he did not

know. Perhaps a pirate, a clown, a magician. He wanted freedom to shape him the way he was meant to be shaped.

Once there was a boy who didn't really exist. Except he did, to one person—a little girl. And when he left to be free, it was only because she allowed it. The boy promised to never forget her—not because he was particularly stubborn, or prone to guilt. He knew it was just plain impossible. Even when winter came, and the light was blunt enough to erase anything, he'd remember. And when the leaves turned black beneath the snow, and when the initials in the tree grew faint over the years. Even when those initials were nearly invisible, and the tree was chopped down to be made into a boat, he would remember.

Once there was a boy who sailed away, unsure what future lay ahead on those dark, unknown waters.

Chapter Thirty-two
DARK

When I opened my eyes, all was dark.

Can an imaginary thing die? I wondered.

Am I in a coma?

Or is this what it feels like to be real?

At first, in the dark, I thought I heard the sound of Fleur calling my name, but it sounded far, far away like an echo, and faded until I could hear nothing at all. I closed my eyes, and then I opened them, but the dark was just the same. Hours passed. At least I think they did; I had no way of really knowing. It may have been days. Or weeks. Or months. For all I knew, I had lived a whole lifetime there in that darkest dark.

And the worst part was that there was nothing for me to do but think. And remember.

I thought about our house. It's a funny thing, a house, the way you memorize every creaky floorboard, every pencil line on the wall measuring height, until it all becomes a part of you without you even noticing. I was sure that even in the deep dark, if I were home, I could still find every wall switch and bring back the light.

I thought about François. I thought about his growls, and nips, and how soft his floppy ears felt when he was snoring and I would sneak a quick pat. What is it with pets? Even the worst ones worm their way into your heart, curl up on a pillow in a slant of warm sunlight, and never leave.

I thought about the way things sounded from a distance—the hum of my father's lawn mower in the summer, the ticking of clocks, the sizzling pans and clicking spoons in the kitchen. I remembered the sound of my parents' voices through the floorboards, like a radio station that didn't quite come in. I could tell worry or joy by their two tones. I thought the sound made a force field around our house, and it always made me feel safe.

And most of all, I remembered the light. I saw the moonlight in our room, the shapes of the sleeping furniture, and the shadow puppets we'd make on the wall. I saw the goldenrod glow on autumn afternoons after school. I saw my mother's curtains, and how their shadows looked like a maze or a puzzle to solve. I saw the light in Fleur's eyes, the color like a pond, with shafts of blue and green; a place where you'd expect a fish to break the surface and leap out at any moment. Have you noticed how a person's eyes get brighter when they talk about something they love? Fleur's eyes lit up like that when she would tell someone about me.

I thought about light.

And missed it.

And wished for it.

Until finally, one day, it came back.

Chapter Thirty-three
FREEDOM?

Finally, I thought, this is what it feels like to be free! The sun was on my face, the wind in my hair. (Except it didn't exactly seem like freedom since I was, technically, tied with heavy rope to the trunk of a large tree.)

"Um, hello?" I said.

"Did I say you could speak?" asked an angry voice.

This, I thought in my delusion, was a good sign: Someone could hear me speak! The only other real person who had ever heard me was Fleur. Therefore, I rationalized, I must now be real to everyone.

From behind the tree stepped a boy, no older than me, with a piece of wood in his hand that he held like a sword.

"I'm the hero," he said. "And you are my prisoner."

"Well a how-do-you-do to you too," I replied. "May I ask how I got here?"

"Probably as a stowaway on a ship after you stole a treasure."

"No," I said. "I don't mean how did my character get here in your little make-believe game. I mean how did I, Jacques Papier, get here in actual real life?"

"Hey," said the boy, his voice now that of a regular, slightly annoyed, eight-year-old. "You can't speak unless I want you to. I imagined you."

And then he hit me with a blow, more painful than any from a wooden sword.

"You," he said, "are my new imaginary friend."

Chapter Thirty-four
THE DUM-DUM BANDITS

And so, it seemed, there had been some grave mistake: I had been set free by Fleur only to be imagined by someone else. And that someone, it turned out, was a particularly deranged individual named Pierre.

On Monday Pierre decided we were bank robbers. First he imagined me as his horse, but I protested so much after changing shape into a horse, he finally compromised and allowed me to be an outlaw like him, complete with snakeskin boots and bandannas over our faces. The only problem was that when we went to rob the bank, the woman inside thought Pierre was *"just the most precious thing"* (her words, not mine), and handed him a lollipop. Pierre proceeded to grab the entire jar of those tiny lollipops and run from the bank, hooting and hollering, making finger-gun motions into the air.

Our "grand heist" aside, I highly doubt the Dum-Dum Bandits will make the evening news.

On Tuesday Pierre said we were pilots, and imagined us in cheesy matching flight suits and helmets. Then he decided our plane was going down fast, and we'd have to eject. Except our plane was a tree, and Pierre-the-genius forgot to imagine we had parachutes, so now we have matching bandages on our heads.

On Wednesday Pierre decided we were zookeepers. We stalked an escaped tiger for about half the day, but it turned out it was just a skittish stray cat from the neighborhood. And let me tell you, Pierre's water gun did the opposite of tranquilizing that wild beast. Of course Pierre dodged the feline rebuttal, but my good ole pal imagined that I was not so lucky. My entire body is now covered in scratches except the part that was already bandaged.

Maybe tomorrow Pierre would imagine me as someone who dies from rabies.

On Thursday, we played storybook and (*of course*) Pierre got to be the valiant prince. What was I? you ask. The dragon?

The knight? Maybe a delightful court jester with zero chance of being maimed or injured? No. Pierre imagined me as the damsel in distress. Me! A damsel! And he couldn't imagine me as a bold, brilliant warrior princess with martial arts skills. Noooooo. He had to belittle my womanly strength along with everything else. Well, my dress may have been frilly and covered in heart-shaped jewels, and my hair may have been prohibitively long, but I was no damsel in distress. I was formulating a plan. Also, as luck would have it, Pierre got called in to dinner by his mom before we got to the part where I was awoken with true love's stinky kiss. Let's just say "Prince Pierre" needs a royal lesson in oral hygiene.

As you can imagine, by Friday, I'd had all I could take. While Pierre was asleep, I gathered up my crown and lacy petticoats, and made my way off into the night.

Chapter Thirty-five
I QUIT!

"*Hubba, hubba,*" said Stinky Sock, winking at me when I walked into the Imaginaries Anonymous meeting.

"There's a free seat next to me, Princess," chimed in Mr. Pitiful.

"I'm not a princess!" I shouted, slumping into the chair, straightening my dress. "I'm a *damsel* in *distress.*"

"*Jacques?*" asked Stinky Sock, his woolen mouth agape. "Is that you?!"

"Yes, of course it's me," I said, burying my face in my hands. "And I *quit!* Can I do that?" I asked, looking up. "Can you quit an imaginary job?"

"Well," said Mr. Pitiful, "you probably can if you get approval, but you'll have to do a lot of paperwork."

"Seriously," I continued. "All jokes aside, you guys have

to help me. Nobody told me that freedom means being imagined by some new kid. And to make matters worse, I'm ninety-nine percent sure that this Pierre kid is the most wanted of the wanteds on *America's Most Wanted*."

"Well, what did you put on your form?" asked Mr. Pitiful. "You must have written something wacky to get placed with such a wacko."

"Form?" I asked. "What form?"

"The placement form," he continued. "At the reassignment office."

"*WHAT REASSIGNMENT OFFICE?!*" I shouted.

The Everything looked around at the other imaginaries, pointed at me, and smiled his chess-piece-and-soda-can smile.

"It's like he's from another planet," he teased. "Oh sorry," he added. "I meant she."

"Everyone knows if you're set free, you have to get reassigned," explained Stinky Sock. "Or else you'll be trapped in dark limbo, and then at the whim of anyone who imagines you as anything they can think of, like some sort of imaginary Silly Putty. Like a paper doll cut into any shape. Like steel forged by the hand of the Great Imaginer. Like—"

"Okay, okay," I said. "Write your epic poem on your own time. And for the record, guys, all this information would have been very useful to me *before* I convinced Fleur to set me free." I stood up, readjusting my petticoats with as much pride as I could muster.

"Now, where is this office?" I asked, shaking my golden locks. "My feet are killing me and I simply must get out of these heels."

Chapter Thirty-six
THE REASSIGNMENT FORM

PERSONAL DATA

Surname: __Papier__   First Name: __Jacques__

Address (former): ____the top bunk bed____

Family Members (former): ____Mom, Dad, Fleur, and__

(ugh!) François the evil wiener dog____

Have you ever been assigned by the Office of Reassignment

in the past (Y/N): _nope_

Are you legally qualified for imaginary employment?

~~maybe? a little?~~ Yes____

GENERAL

Days Available:

☐ Monday   ☐ Thursday   ☐ Sunday

☐ Tuesday   ☐ Friday   ☐ Funday

☐ Wednesday   ☐ Saturday

Employment Category:

☐ Full-time imaginary friend   ☐ Full-time imaginary nemesis

SPECIALIZED SKILLS (check all that apply)

☐ Flight

☐ Pie making

☐ Tree climbing

☐ Cloud shaping

☐ Pie eating

☐ Piracy (high seas)

☐ Evaporation

☐ Glow in the dark

☐ Roller skating

☐ Liquification

☐ Super strength

☐ Karaoke

☐ Tap dancing

☐ Mind reading

☐ High-shelf-reaching

☐ Guessing wrapped gifts

☐ Impeccable manners

☐ Unicycling

☐ Making echoes

☐ Growing extra arms

☐ Hearing seashells

☐ Breathing fire

☐ Math homework

☐ Microsoft Word

ONE FINAL QUESTION

Is there any other information you would like us to consider?

_____

_____

_____

_____

Chapter Thirty-seven
THE OFFICE OF REASSIGNMENT

"I have no skills!" I shouted, tossing my form aside in a fit of exasperation.

The reassignment officer behind the desk gave me a look of disgust, then made a few marks on the clipboard in her hands.

"Anxiety, rudeness, and poor self-esteem," she said under her breath as she wrote.

The officer wore glasses on a chain that kept getting tangled in her arms, but she still seemed to be getting a large amount of work done. This was most likely due to the fact that she had been imagined with not two but eight tentacle arms that were constantly moving and writing in every direction. That was good, since the office was stacked to the ceiling with files and papers. Or maybe it just seemed that

way because the room was so small. The Office of Reassignment was always moving, I'd been told, and was currently
located in a large cardboard box in a yard full of toys.

"Sometimes the kids imagine it's a spaceship," explained
the reassignment officer. "Other times a candy house,
dragon cave, mud-pie factory, school for monsters, or run-
away choo-choo train," she continued. "Packed in every fiber
with imagination, these kinds of places."

"Would it be possible," I asked the officer, "for me to just
go back to Fleur, the girl who originally imagined me? She
set me free, but only because I asked her. She'd be *thrilled* to
have me back."

"*Thrilled*, I'm sure," said the officer with what I sensed
was sarcasm. "But no. I'm running your paperwork through
the system now."

"But . . ." I started to say. "I didn't get to answer the last
part yet . . ."

Too late. A machine that looked as if it was made of old
toilet paper rolls beep-bopped as it ate up my paperwork.
After a moment of consideration, it spit out a wee card.

"Very well," said the secretary. "When you leave this
office out that door"— she motioned to a flap of cardboard

that looked like a doggy door—"you'll be at your new destination. Thank you for choosing this branch of the Imaginary Office of Reassignment, and have a very nonexistent day."

As I got down on my knees to crawl out the door to my new home, I thought about the last conversation I'd had with Stinky Sock before I'd left Imaginaries Anonymous.

"It was horrible," I'd told him. "Changing shape again and again with Pierre. It made it perfectly clear how utterly unreal I am."

"Eh, shapes." Stinky Sock shrugged the best he could without shoulders. "Even kids change shape eventually—get bigger, older, spottier, wrinklier, stooped over in old age like a fading flower. I wouldn't worry about it too much. Spend less time thinking of that, and more time thinking about what's in *there*."

The sock pointed to my chest, where my heart would be if it turned out I had one.

"Why? What do *you* think is in there?" I asked.

"I don't know," said my friend. "But don't you think it's high time you found out?"

Chapter Thirty-eight
THE THING I HATE MOST

What was inside me, I learned after crawling through the doggy door, was the thing I hate most.

Allow me to explain.

After I left the Office of Reassignment, I emerged into a cage. As soon as I entered, the door I'd come in through disappeared, trapping me in some sort of prison.

"What are other people writing on their forms?" I shouted. "Is there some sort of manual I could read?"

I decided to breathe, not panic, and take stock of the situation.

1. I could smell about a zillion different smells.

2. My hearing seemed to have greatly improved, as if the world were in surround

sound. I watched a small beetle walk at the edge of the enclosure and could actually hear its steps.

3. I must have become a superhero.

4. Or another damsel in distress, locked in a tower . . .

5. I was very itchy. Like covered-in-bug-bites-after-playing-outside-on-a-summer-night itchy.

6. I was either a superhero or a princess with a rash.

7. There were lots of dogs in this prison.

8. Was it possible to be imagined *by* a dog?

9. Did dogs even have imaginations?

10. Uh-oh, people approaching . . .

The group was made up of a man in a stained uniform, a husband and wife, and a pigtailed girl in a pretty white dress who was bouncing off the walls and running from cage to cage. She looked like a moth in a lightbulb factory. She looked like a frog at a fly family reunion.

"And that one is so SPOTTY!!" she shouted. "And that one is so big! And look at the ears! And the wagging tail. Do  you think that one is soft? And look at that one's WITTLE BITTY FACE! Ahhhhhhh!!"

"I told you this was a bad idea," the woman said to the man. "She's not responsible enough for a dog." Then more loudly to the girl: "Remember, Merla, sweetie, we're just *visiting*."

"I WANT THEM ALLLLLLLLL!!" shouted the girl in reply, running up and down the aisles of cages like a bee in a botanical garden.

Merla stopped outside my enclosure and, to my surprise, pointed right at me.

"That," she said in a reverent tone, "is the dog I want."

"Who are you calling a dog, kid?" I asked.

"EEEEeeeeeeeeEEEEeeeeeee!!" screamed Merla. "It can TALK!"

"Oh. Oh man, oh geez," I said, the reality knocking me upside the head. (Or should I say snout.)

"I'm a *dog* now, aren't I?"

The girl's parents joined her outside my enclosure. They looked at each other, then at Merla, then at me. Well, sort of at me. They were actually looking at the opposite end of the cage.

"Of course," said Merla's father in a false, grand voice. "You can have as many dogs from *that* cage as you want, button."

"There's only one," replied Merla. "One perfect dog. Gimme, gimme, gimme!"

Now the parents stared at the slovenly kennel keeper. *Well,* their look said. *Give the kid her invisible dog.*

The kennel keeper, clearly unsure what to do, made a big pantomime show of unlocking my cage. He swept his arm as if to present me, then said in a robotic voice, "Look. It is a dog. In this cage. You may take him now."

And so, Merla ran inside the enclosure, scooped me up in her arms, and squeezed me so hard that—oh, the embarrassment to admit it!—well, I took an imaginary piddle right there on her pretty white dress.

Chapter Thirty-nine
MERLA + DOG 4-EVER

Once we arrived in Merla's bedroom, I realized she might have an ever-so-slight obsession with dogs: There were food and water bowls, chew toys, posters, Milk-Bones, a frilly doggy bed, and even a scrapbook with the words MERLA + DOG 4-EVER printed in a heart on the front cover.

"A bit non-specific, don't you think?" I grabbed a marker, crossed out DOG and in its place wrote JACQUES PAPIER: TEMPORARY DOG.

"Oh. My. Gosh," said Merla, mesmerized. "You can *write* too?"

"Of course I can write," I said, puffing up my chest. "The English teacher may not have been able to see me, but in my opinion, I was top of my class in the second grade in both spelling *and* cursive writing."

"A dog who can do cursive writing," said Merla, shaking her head. "I really hit the jackpot."

I started poking around, taking stock of my new belongings.

"That," I said, pointing to a bone, "is not going to work for me. I'll eat what you eat. I also enjoy warm bubble baths and classical music, and for some reason I feel I'd like you to scratch behind my ear."

Merla leaned over and scratched the exact right place. Not bad.

"Anything else?" she asked.

"Yes," I said. "I'd like to know what I look like."

"I could take a photo with Daddy's camera," she offered.

"That won't work. Sadly, they've yet to invent film or a mirror that captures imaginary things. No, Merla, you hyperactive fool," I said, pushing a box of crayons in her direction. "You're going to have to draw me."

"Fun!" said Merla. "Where do you want to pose?"

I looked around.

"Here," I said, languishing across my frilly dog bed like I'd seen in old paintings of fancy women at the museum.

"And make sure you capture my good side," I said. "That is, if I still have one."

Chapter Forty
A PORTRAIT OF JACQUES PAPIER

When Merla the *artiste* finished the drawing, she held it up to admire, then turned it around with dramatic flair. I stood up from the bed and moved closer for inspection.

It's an odd thing, I thought, only being able to see yourself through someone else's eyes. My denial had been so deep with Fleur, I had never registered the fact that I didn't show up in mirrors or photos. But I had finally come to terms with the reality of my situation.

"Merla," I asked. "Would you say you've had . . . much experience with this medium?"

"Crayons?" asked Merla. "Oh sure. Just look, half these colors are worn right down to nubs."

"Well then, are you going through some sort of Picasso phase? Is this your banana period? Because looking at these

MƎRLA

ratios . . . I mean, I hate to critique, but the legs are far too short, and it almost looks as if my stomach would drag on the . . ." I stopped. I stared. I stuttered. "On the, uh . . . the ground," I finished.

My heart started to drum. The beats said the same word: *Fran-çois, Fran-çois, Fran-çois.*

I am, I realized, what I hate most.

I am wiener dog.

Chapter Forty-one
IMAGINARY EMERGENCY

I waited until Merla was snoring, loosened her vise-like grip from around my neck, and sneaked down the street to a pay phone. On the way I passed a sign on the ground, fallen from a telephone pole. LOST: ONE IMAGINARY FRIEND. CALL PIERRE.

I shuddered, kept my head down, and continued walking.

When I reached the phone booth, I climbed onto my hind legs on the small seat inside, put my quarter into the slot, and dialed the number for the Imaginary Office of Reassignment. An automated voice answered, and began listing options.

You have reached the after-hours emergency line for the Office of Reassignment. Please listen carefully, as our menu has changed.

Press 1 if you have been imagined as a houseplant.

Press 2 if you have been imagined as a trademarked character and are worried about legal issues.

Press 3 if you have been imagined as a cloud on a windy day.

Press 4 if you have been imagined as a ghost.

Press 5 if . . .

I leaned my head against the cool side of the phone booth and closed my eyes, listening to what seemed to be an endless list of possible imaginary emergencies.

Press 26 if you have been imagined as food and are about to be eaten.

Press 55 if you have been imagined as a figure made of sand and the water is lapping at your feet.

Press 99 if you have been imagined as the thing you hate most—

"It's about time!" I yelled, pressing the nine key twice. After a few rings, a sleepy voice came on the line.

"Hello, what is your imaginary emergency?"

"I've been imagined as a wiener dog!" I shouted into the phone.

"Okay, calm down," said the receptionist. "Let me get the emergency dog intake sheet. Question one: Is your new child abusive?"

"No," I answered.

"Is your new child forcing you to eat dog food?"

"No."

"Fetch against your will?"

"No."

"Is your new child trying to ride you like a horse?"

"No! None of that," I said. "Merla is actually quite sweet. I just personally hate wiener dogs."

"Well, you must have put something on your form to get this assignment," said the voice, sounding more bored by the minute.

"I wrote down that I used to *live* with an evil wiener dog named François," I explained. "But that was clearly not a *preference*."

"Ah," said the specialist. "That must be it. The system just does a keyword search. Probably picked up on it."

"Oh *good*," I said sarcastically. "What a *wonderful* system. How could a machine constructed from imagination and toilet paper rolls work so *well*. Regardless," I continued, "I will still be needing a new assignment."

"Actually, sir, since this isn't a real emergency, you'll have to wait until Monday. And even then, there's roughly a zero percent chance this case will qualify for a transfer. Have a very nonexistent weekend. Buh-bye now."

Can you believe it? She hung up on me. In my time of need! My hour of crisis!

I felt, dare I say it, lower than a wiener dog.

Chapter Forty-two
BELLY RUBS AND LIGHTNING BUGS

I made my way back to Merla's house, trying my best not to howl at the moon with frustration. I passed by a swing set on the way, and a memory of the day I met Cowgirl in the park floated through my mind. How I'd whined! And about what, really? About having a loving sister, and sweet parents, and the best life ever? What a fool I'd been.

I decided to take a little ride, but it took all my effort just to get my front paws on the swaying swing and haul myself onto the seat. Even then I just hung across it on my stomach like a limp hoagie left out in the rain.

So much for the swings, I thought. So much for a lot of things from my old life.

Over the next days the only benefit I could find to being a dog—and trust me it did *not* make it worth it—was that I could do all the messy things Fleur and I were always told not to back home. I rolled in the sweet-smelling grass, tumbled in a mud puddle, and caught lightning bugs in my mouth to see what light tastes like. (It tastes like chicken.) Plus I was closer to the ground, so I could smell the dew, join a march of ants, and feel the sunshine stored in the dirt.

I continued making the best of being Merla's dog until the day I overheard her parents conversing in the kitchen while they put away the groceries.

"Did you buy the flea bath?" asked Merla's mother.

"Yes," said her father, sighing. "But doesn't it seem a tad wasteful to bathe imaginary fleas off an imaginary dog?"

"Actually," replied Merla's mother, "I think she's showing great responsibility. If she keeps this up, I think it might be time for a *real* dog."

Now, *a real dog* may have been the words they said, sure. But what I heard was: *That's my ticket out of here.*

Chapter Forty-three
THE DOG ~~ATE~~ DID MY HOMEWORK

And so Responsibility became my middle name. Jacques R. Papier, wiener dog extraordinaire, at your service. All I had to do was get Merla to go along with it, which wasn't hard once I told her there might be a *real* dog in it for her.

"You can do this," I told her. "You've got the energy. The spunk. You're like a human wind-up toy! I'll even help."

And so every day I'd wait at the window for Merla to come home from school, and then we'd get to work.

"I washed Jacques Papier the wiener dog today," said Merla to her parents at dinner. "I also dried him, combed his hair, cut his toenails, brushed his teeth, and tweezed his eyebrows."

"Wow," said her father, taking a bite of his pork chop. "I didn't even know dogs *had* eyebrows."

The next day Merla found her mother in the living room.

"I did all the laundry," said Merla, hauling a bin half her size across the floor. "I cleaned it, hung it, and folded it. I even hand-washed the delicates."

"Well . . . thank you, sweetie," said Merla's mother, a look on her face as if her daughter had just grown a second head.

"And Dad," Merla added, turning to her father, who was reading a book, "I shined your shoes, took out the trash, and cleaned the gutters."

"That's amazing," said her father, dumbfounded.

"Oh, also," said Merla as she left the room, "I changed the oil in your car."

When she turned the corner, I slapped Merla a high (lowish) five.

"Now," I said, "on to schoolwork. Do you have any extra we could do? Do you have your books for next year yet?"

And wouldn't you know it, when Merla handed in her

homework that week, she reported back to me that she'd gotten all A-plus-plus-*pluses*.

I have to admit, it felt pretty good. Even her teacher had been in awe.

"Quite the improvement," said Merla's teacher. "I'm wondering, what changed?"

"Oh that's easy," said Merla. "My dog did my homework."

Chapter Forty-four
THE BEST DOG EVER

And then, one day—one glorious day—Merla's father walked in the door with a box. And not just any box, but one with a red bow on top and air holes cut in the sides. I knew it could only mean one thing.

When Merla opened it, I expected her to scream, or shout, or for her head to pop off like the top of a dandelion. But to my great surprise, she gently lifted the scrappy mutt from the box and kissed him on the forehead. She was calm and quiet in her joy. She let him sniff her hand, and was totally patient while he got comfy and fell asleep. She was, all in all, an A-plus-plus-*plus* caretaker for a real pet.

"Cute dog," I said. "Good choice. Not too oblong at all."

But Merla wasn't listening. She was far, far away in the warm land of real puppy heaven.

I made my way to the bedroom. There I packed my few canine belongings, including the crayon drawing of me that Merla had made, and walked out into the hall.

"Well," I said loudly, my voice echoing off the wood floors and walls. "I guess I'll be going. No more need for me here."

I assumed now that Merla had a real dog, I was free to leave. Just like I'd wanted.

"Good-bye," I said.

It's strange, but without someone to hear it, that word sounded more empty and small than just about any other. But before I could fully squeeze my body out the doggy door, I heard quick footsteps and felt a hand on my back.

"It's okay if you want to leave," said Merla, "now that the puppy is here. You never really loved being my dog, did you?"

"Aw, shucks." I smiled. "It wasn't all bad."

"Before you go," said Merla, "wanna hear why I love dogs so much?"

"Honestly, I would," I said. "I've only known one, and he was the worst."

"What I like about a dog," said Merla, "is that a dog doesn't care if you're hyperactive, or weird-looking, or the dumbest person at multiplication in your whole class. They don't care if you get your dress muddy, or can never tell jokes quite right, or if you're the least popular kid in third grade. A dog will still wait for you to come home every day. And always be excited to see you. A great dog thinks you're the best person in the entire world.

"But you know what are the *best* dogs?" asked Merla. "They're the ones that make you feel like you can do anything. I mean, how many *people* in the world ever believe in you that way? See something in you, and make you feel special?"

"Hardly any," I agreed. "Maybe one or two along the way, if you're lucky."

"Well, you know what, Jacques Papier, temporary dog?" asked Merla.

"What?" I asked.

"You," she said, smiling her great, wild smile, "were the best dog ever."

Chapter Forty-five
THE THINGS I'M GOING TO MISS

I found myself, once again, waiting in the Office of Reassignment. While I waited I replayed Merla's words over and over in my head.

The best dog ever.

I can't tell you what those words meant to me. That's because I can't even tell myself what they meant to me, or why they were so important.

The best dog ever.

The last time I felt so special was when I was with Fleur. It was a feeling, I realized, that I wanted to give back. I had actually *liked* helping Merla; to my surprise, I had actually liked it better than helping myself. Had Merla's words held some magic?

All I knew was how good they felt, and that everyone—

even if you don't happen to be a dog—should try saying those words, maybe just to yourself, or maybe out loud, eyes closed, until you really believe it.

"*I am the best dog ever.*"

Go ahead. Try it.

"*I am the best dog ever.*"

"I don't know about the best, but you're certainly a very *oblong* dog, that's for certain."

I opened my eyes, the trance broken.

"Is it really you?" I asked. I jumped up and tackled the Roller-Skating Cowgirl, licking her face until she pet my ears.

"Well, a howdy-do to you too, Jacques Papier," said Cowgirl.

Then it dawned on me where we both were, and what that meant. "So if you're at the Office of Reassignment, then . . ."

"Then my little girl let me go," finished Cowgirl. "It's true."

"How are you holding up?" I asked.

"Oh, you know," said Cowgirl. "It's hard. I can't help thinking about all the things I'm going to miss, all the things I'll never get to see. She has her first school dance next week. I know she wouldn't have let me join her or anything, but I still would have liked to see her in a dress just the same. You know, I've never seen her in anything but overalls and cowboy boots."

I thought about this for a moment. I thought about Fleur, and how she had asked me to never forget her, to come back if I could.

"I think you will be there," I said, putting my paw on Cowgirl's hand. "She imagined you. Which makes you part of her. I think that lasts for always."

Cowgirl dried her eyes and tried to smile.

"Maybe you're right," she said, patting my head. "Thanks, pardner. I guess maybe you really are the best lil' doggy ever there was."

After Cowgirl set out to her new assignment, I ran into a most unwelcome former acquaintance.

"Cheerio, young chap. If you're here at the reassignment office, you must have taken my advice."

"You!" I shouted, pointing my paw at the Oogly Boogly. "You *tricked* me!"

"Oh?" said the Oogly Boogly. He sipped a cup of tea with his pinky extended from the cup and dripping smoke onto the floor.

"I just wanted answers," I replied. "To know what I am.

And you tricked me into all this. I have every right to be angry with you."

"Angry, eh?" he asked. "To me you seem *scared*."

The Oogly Boogly leaned in. I could smell all the fear he had caused the children who had imagined him.

"And I," he continued, "*know* scared."

"S-scared?" I stuttered. "Scared of *what*?"

"Maybe," said the Oogly Boogly, "you are solving the question of what you really are. And maybe, just maybe, you don't like the answer."

Chapter Forty-six
THE PETRIFIED PRAIRIE DOG

After my much more carefully completed paperwork was processed, I gladly bid farewell to the Oogly Boogly and walked through the door and into my new assignment, ready to prove I wasn't scared of anything. It was a regular old living room in a regular old house. The first thing I saw was a head disappearing behind a sofa. The head had a mop of sandy hair and thick glasses, and it reminded me of a petrified prairie dog ducking into a burrow.

"Uh, hello?" I said.

At this, the figure behind the sofa raced down the hall, opened a door, and went inside with a slam. I followed, and knocked, and when nobody answered, tried again. Finally after my third try, the door slowly creaked open a few inches.

"Greetings," I said, finally face-to-face with the little owl eyes behind the glasses. "I'm Jacques Papier. Pleasure to meet you."

I put out my hand to shake, but the boy covered his head like I was going to clobber him.

"Do you have a name?" I asked. The boy did not reply, but I saw a name written in marker on a backpack hanging on the closet door.

"Here's the thing, *Bernard*," I said. "I get the sense you'd like me to go away, but that's going to be hard since you're the one imagining me."

At this news, Bernard's eyes got even wider, if possible. I was about to ask Bernard what he had imagined me to look like, when we heard a man's voice call from the kitchen.

"Dinnertime, Bernie! And please wash your hands if you're hiding in the closet again."

In reply, Bernard ran past me toward the kitchen as if his hair was on fire.

Not the best manners on that petrified prairie dog, if you ask me. This, I thought, was not going to be any fun.

Chapter Forty-seven
YIMELLO

I joined Bernard and his father at the table. Bernard's dad wore glasses just like his son, and had several leaky pens in the front pocket of his shirt.

"So champ, how are you?" asked the father.

"How am I?" I said. "The better question would be *what* am I . . . oh." I stopped. "You meant him."

Bernard was staring at me across the table with his unblinking eyes.

"So in my class," his father began, "my students are learning that the human eye has millions of light-sensitive cells called cones. They are what enable us to see colors."

That explained the glasses and pens. Bernard's dad was a professional nerd.

"Dogs only have two cone types," his father prattled on,

(professional nerd)

heaping peas onto his son's plate. "So they can see shades of green and blue." I watched the pea-steam fog up Bernard's glasses.

Without taking his eyes off me, Bernard picked up his fork full of peas and slowly brought it toward his face. By the time the fork got there, no peas were left, and I'm fairly certain he would have poked his eye out had it not been for his glasses.

"Humans," continued Bernard's dad like a science book, "have three kinds of cones. So we see green, blue, and red. Butterflies have five kinds.

"But the best eyes," continued Bernard's dad, "belong to one special kind of shrimp. Those shrimp have sixteen cones. Can you believe that?

"So the rainbow we see is just made from the color combinations of green, blue, and red. Now, imagine what the rainbow would look like to that little shrimp! It would be huge, and vast, and have infrared, and ultraviolet, and things we can't even imagine. And the thing is, they're technically

looking at the same thing we are. The stuff they can see just—"

"Invisible to us," said Bernard, finishing the sentence.

Bernard's father smiled in shock. He stopped speaking, looking as if he'd just gotten a wild animal to eat from his hand but wasn't going to push his luck.

After dinner, I sat alone with Bernie, who continued his unblinking stare.

"I've got noooowhere to be, kid," I said, narrowing my eyes, staring back. "I can do this all night."

"Yimello," said Bernard finally, breaking the silence.

"Gesundheit?" I asked.

"It's a name for one of the colors that's invisible to us. Yimello," said Bernard. "There could also be glowl and novaly and replitz."

"Yes." I nodded, stunned the kid could actually string together so many words at once. "And, uh, don't forget the beautiful grynn, the luminous dulloff, or the subtle winooze."

Bernard's face lit up. He stood and started pacing the room, speaking quickly. "Or salty, and insomnia, and care-free, and talkative, and lonely, and burnt, and punctual."

"Some of my favorite colors," I agreed, nodding. "We

could paint this room whisper. Or zigzag. Or maybe a nice shade of ignored and invisible."

Bernard couldn't help it, and let out a quiet, gasping sort of laugh.

"Holy hilarity," he added.

I admit it, I laughed too. What can I say? The kid was actually pretty funny.

But this, I would learn, was just one of Bernard's many colors that nobody else ever got to see.

Chapter Forty-eight
NO WORD

That night I slept in a sleeping bag in Bernard's room. I lay there, wide-awake, looking at the square of light on the floor made by the moon. I thought about the words Bernie and I had made up earlier, and how that was good, because when you really thought about it, there weren't enough words in the world. There was not, I realized, a word for a square of light on a floor made by the moon.

There's also no word for when you're about to introduce someone and then just forget their name. Everyone has felt that little pang of panic, and yet there's no word for it.

And there's no word for secret messages in alphabet soup.

Or the first time you put bare feet in the grass after a long winter.

Or when a dog climbs up onto your bed, wags his tail, and smacks you upside the head with happiness.

Or when your hair looks way worse after a haircut.

Or when someone has a smile that looks so lit up, there must be a lightning bug caught in their head. (For the record, I would petition this word be called Fleur.)

There's no word for that old trick where you tap someone on the opposite shoulder from behind to fool them.

Or for a stranger's note in a used book.

There's no word for when someone hilarious and weird like Bernard decides it's better to be the most invisible boy in the world instead of being teased. I suppose it had its comforts, not existing. Like being airy, drifting along, being able to go in and out of a place, unnoticed. Having no friends, and therefore nobody to ever lose.

There's no word for ships that want to stay sunken, needles that hide in the haystack, or pearls that are buried forever beneath the sand.

"You know, Bernie," I said to him one day as several people cut in front of us in line at the movies. "It's slightly insulting to someone like me who is *actually* invisible that you would try so hard not to be seen."

It probably wasn't something anyone else would notice, but being invisible myself, I was especially attuned. There was the way he always hung his pictures in art class so that each one was hidden behind someone else's, or how he dressed in bland, blah colors, or the way he moved so silently, it seemed as if his feet were made of dandelion puffs.

There's no word for the way Bernard hid his real self like a squirrel stowing away nuts for winter.

"Once," he said, "I was so invisible that a bird—an actual *bird*—landed on my head. I thought she might go ahead and make a nest."

There's certainly no word, I thought, for someone who seems like a fitting home for birds.

Chapter Forty-nine
THE LOBSTER STRIKES

Bernard may have been able to stay invisible forever if it weren't for the day he almost blinded a girl in his class.

It was gym period, outdoors, and they were playing the most feared game of any bespectacled student: dodgeball. Actually, at Bernard's school they didn't call it that, because there were too many hedges and bushes near the court, so they called it lodge ball or hedge ball, but never dodgeball. Bernard employed what he explained was his "usual tactic."

"Okay, you hide in the bushes. And then what?" I asked.

"And then I wait for gym to be over, obviously," replied Bernard in a "duh" tone.

"But it's supposed to be fun," I said. "It's a playground."

"Have you ever *been* on a playground?" asked Bernard. "It's lawless! It's anarchy! It's *only-the-person-holding-the-*

128

conch-shell-can-speak-and-let's-kill-the-kid-in-glasses."

"Wow. Graphic," I replied.

The system probably would have worked if, after everyone on Bernard's team had been eliminated, someone hadn't spotted a flash of red shoelace behind a bush.

"Hey, we have someone left!" Bernard's team cried.

Bernard peeked his owl eyes around the edge of the bush.

"Who is that?"

"Does he even go to school here?"

"I think it's just a large rodent."

But no. It was Bernard, who was forced to come out from hiding and join the game. Every single red playground ball was on his side of the court, several stuck in the very bush he'd been using for shelter. Gingerly, he picked one up, and pushed his glasses up his nose.

"H-holy horrifying s-situation," he stuttered.

It was a fair assessment, for his opponents were many:

There was a boy known on the dodgeball courts as the Trombone because of his freakishly long arms, resulting in slingshot throws and shocking catches. There was Midnight Blue, a girl so small and quick, you never saw her coming. And finally, most dreaded of all, the Henhouse. It was a mystery of science how that boy held so many balls in his hands at once, but he could carry half a dozen as if they were small as chicken eggs.

"What you need to do," I told him, "is take a ball in each hand."

Bernard did as I said. I stood and looked him over.

"The Lobster," I said after a moment.

"What?" asked Bernard.

"That can be your player identity. The red balls look like lobster claws."

"Who cares!" snapped Bernard. "What do I do?!"

"Maybe go for one of the lazier kids in the back," I suggested. "Look! There's a group of girls that have been gossiping the whole game. Try for one of them. They aren't even looking."

"I can't," whispered a panicked Bernard. "One of them is the girl with the freckles."

"Uh, so?" I said. "Aim for a freckle."

"No," he replied. "I just think . . . she's nice."

"Nice?!" I blurted. "Who cares if she's . . . Oooooh, I get it," I smirked, finally catching on. "You have a huge, honking, monster crush on her, don't you?"

"She doesn't even know I exist," answered Bernard.

"Stop whispering to imaginary teammates and play the game!" shouted a voice from the sidelines.

And so Bernard gingerly approached the team divider line painted in white on the playground. I approached the line with him, hoping at least one of us would avoid certain death.

"Float like a rubber butterfly," I coached. "Sting like a plastic bee."

Bernard gritted his teeth. His glasses only magnified the determined look in his eyes. As he released the ball, time slowed, the planets aligned, and then . . .

Bernard actually *hit* someone.

The ball had left the Lobster's claw and connected with . . .

"Holy harm's way," gasped Bernard. "I hit her right in the face!"

It was true. Across the line, Bernard's crush was clutching both hands over her eye as her teammates and teacher ran toward her.

"Well," I tried to comfort Bernard, patting him on the back, "at least now she definitely knows you exist."

Chapter Fifty
FARFALLINI!

Bernard and I stood below the window of the nurse's office. I peered over the sill and through the glass to get a better look at the situation inside.

"See," I said, crouching back down to join Bernard. "I told you she'd be fine. She's just sitting there with an ice pack over her eye. If it were anything serious, there would be an ambulance or a priest or something."

"Phew," said Bernard. "So I guess I should go apologize?"

"Whoa, whoa, whoa," I said, stopping Bernard. "Cool your jets, Casanova. Do you even know what you're going to say to this girl?"

"How about 'Sorry I maimed you by throwing a ball at your face'?" answered Bernard.

"No, that's too boring," I explained. "Man, you're so lucky

you have me. If you're going to talk to a girl, first you have to have some topics of conversation. You know, things you have in common with her."

"I don't know what we have in common," said Bernard.

"Well, what are your favorite things?" I asked. "We'll just find one that everyone likes and mention that. For example," I continued, "what's your favorite animal?"

"Seahorses," replied Bernard without hesitation.

"Do you want to take a minute to think about it?" I asked. "No? Okay, seahorses it is," I said. "How about, what are your favorite hobbies?"

"I like making mud pies," said Bernard.

"Not romantic."

"I like peeling corn when we have corn for dinner," tried Bernard.

"Peeling corn is not a hobby."

"I like collecting feathers."

"Gross."

"I'd like to be a magician. Alakazam! Holy Houdini!"

"Please never tell that to a girl."

"I like making up songs," tried Bernard.

"Okay, good," I said finally. "Music. Everyone loves music."

"Yeah," said Bernard. "I like making up songs about different kinds of pasta. FARFALLINI," he sang. "FUSILLI, SPAGHETTI, RIGATONI, MANICOTTI!"

"Okay, okay, stop please," I said, rubbing my head. "New plan. You go in, I'll stay here outside the window. I'll feed you lines."

"That seems sort of dishonest," replied Bernard.

"When you're wooing a girl," I said, forcing Bernard toward the door, "it's always a good idea to use your imagination."

Chapter Fifty-one
HAVE YOU BEEN THERE THIS WHOLE TIME?

Bernard entered the nurse's office in usual Bernard fashion: like a ghost who just realized he left the house not wearing pants. He creepily crept through the doorway without the nurse even noticing, then slipped around a shelf of brochures about head lice and the dangers of not flossing. He slid so stealthily, and so quietly, that when the girl with the freckles (and black eye) finally saw him, she yelped out in surprise.

"Ack!" she shouted. "Sorry," she added, recovering once she realized that Bernard was just a harmless Bernard. "Have you been there this whole time?"

No reply from Bernard.

"I'm Zoë," she said.

I tried to Jedi-mind-force Bernard to say his name, but he just stood there with his mouth open like one of those clowns you shoot water into at the fair. Any minute now, I was sure his balloon brain would burst.

"Say," continued Zoë, "aren't you the one who hit me in the eye?"

This time, in reply, Bernard turned red and tried to shrink behind the privacy curtain next to Zoë's bed. I figured it was time for me to step in before Bernard ended up with a black eye as well.

"Psssssst," I whispered.

Bernard looked toward the window.

"No, don't look at me!" I shouted.

Bernard jerked his head back toward Zoë, then toward the floor, then the ceiling.

"Say something about the game," I coached.

"Should I say I'm sorry?" whispered Bernard. He wasn't looking at the window, but he also wasn't looking at Zoë. He was, much like a lunatic, speaking to the floor.

"Are you asking *me*?" replied Zoë.

"Tell her . . ." I tried to come up with something poetic. "Tell her that her hair is the color of freshly peeled corn.

That her eyes are like mud pies. That her freckles are like a connect-the-dot that makes the shape of your heart."

"No!" cried Bernard. "I'm not going to say that!"

"Fine, then *don't* apologize," replied Zoë, crossing her arms. "Geez Louise."

I slapped my hand over my face. We were going to have to take this show on the road. Just then the school nurse came over to check on Zoë, took the ice pack off, and inspected the damage.

"Because of the scratch," she said, "you'll have to wear this for a few days." The nurse handed Zoë a black medical eye patch. The kind a pirate would wear.

"I called your mother, she'll be here soon," continued the nurse. "Just rest until then."

The nurse reached behind her to get a pillow for Zoë, and yelped.

"Ack!" she shouted, nearly stepping on Bernard.

"Sorry," the nurse apologized. "Have you been there this whole time?"

Holy hopeless, I thought. This was going to be harder than I'd realized.

Chapter Fifty-two
BABY BERNIE'S FIRST COHERENT SENTENCE

I convinced Bernard to walk to Zoë's house after school with a bouquet of dandelions, the stems limp in his nervous hands. It was the civilized thing to do, especially after he (fine, *we*) had made such a mess out of the first apology.

"You again?" said Zoë. Her mother had convinced her to come to the door even though Zoë had protested, afraid someone outside would see her eye patch.

"Are you here to not apologize some more?" she asked Bernard.

Bernard just stood there staring. I elbowed him in the ribs.

"Ow," he whispered, giving me a dirty look. Finally, he mustered his courage, reached into his pocket, and pulled out the eye patch. It was black and plastic, part of a pirate costume from last Halloween. Bernard took off his glasses, placed the patch over his left eye, and put his glasses back on. He then made a sheepish *TA-DA!* motion with his hands.

At first, I thought Zoë might punch him, thinking he was mocking her. But then I saw the tiniest glimmer of laughter in her one good eye. It had worked! We were smooth. We were slick. They would one day write sonnets about the debonair duo! And if not, I'd write them myself.

"Come on, weirdo," said Zoë, grabbing Bernard by the hand. "You can help me with my project."

As Bernard let Zoë lead him inside, he turned and gave me a look that said it all: He was finally being seen.

And he was terrified. So, even though I was a bit of a third wheel, I decided I should probably tag along.

Zoë's family had a pool out back surrounded by plants and rocks, with a small waterfall as well.

"Swanky," I noted. "Who wants a piña colada?"

I was trying to come up with something for Bernard to say—something about fate, destiny, and the path of a dodgeball—when, to my surprise, Bernard actually *spoke*. All on his own. I felt like a puppeteer whose marionette had just stood up and started dancing a jig.

"What sparkly that is thing?" he asked.

Okay, so the words weren't *perfectly* in order. Still, a good effort.

"Oh, my friends and I are doing a dance routine in the talent show," explained Zoë. She held up a hat covered from back to brim in overlapping green sequins.

"Looks like a mermaid tail," said Bernard. "You know, not a lot of people are aware of this, but eye patches give you the ability to see mermaids."

Great. Perfect. Bernard had finally successfully strung together his first coherent sentence around a girl and it was insane.

"Uh, mermaids?" asked Zoë.

"Yeah," said Bernard. "You just have to cover your one good eye to see them."

Zoë laughed. And to my shock, she reached up and covered her one good eye.

"Where mermaids live looks a bit like your pool," said Bernard. "Except they build houses out of whale bones and the wreckage of sunken ships. They play chess with seahorses. They wear capes of fish scales and sleep on beds made from seaweed."

As we listened, I thought I heard a slight splashing from the far end of the pool.

"At night," Bernard continued, "they turn on an electric eel for a night-light, and they light a fire, and the smoke goes up a chimney made from coral."

"Wait a minute," interrupted Zoë, clearly immersed in Bernard's description. "If they live underwater, how could they have a fire?"

"You should ask *them*," said Bernard.

Zoë and I opened our eyes.

Now, look, I know the light was just playing tricks on us. And I know we'd all probably inhaled too much sequin glue. But for the briefest moment, the blue of Zoë's pool gave way to deeper, darker aqua-colored water. The few plants and rocks were replaced with a lagoon and a waterfall where several mermaids lounged half in the water, half in the sun. They splashed and dove, their laughter making the same sound as the water.

Well, then. When it came to imagination, perhaps Bernard was a bit of a magician after all.

Chapter Fifty-three
THE HIDDEN PARTS

After Bernard went to sleep that night, I decided to take a walk and do some thinking. The thing I realized after the instance with the mermaids was that Bernard wasn't just scared, or shy, or auditioning for the part of the cheese in the "Farmer in the Dell." In truth, he just lived in his own private world. *The World of Bernie.* This, I thought, was why the bees and birds landed on him—he clearly had a whole world inside him with rivers of honey and a heart made from flowers. Bernard was just like a closed bud, an acorn with a tree inside, a song yet to be heard.

To tell the truth, I was beginning to think you would be in awe of *anyone* if you saw the parts of them that no one else gets to see. If you could watch them making up little songs, and doing funny faces in the mirror; if you saw them high-fiving a leaf on a tree, or stopping to watch a green inch-worm hanging midair from an invisible thread, or just being really different and lonely and crying sometimes at night. Seeing them, the *real* them, you couldn't help but think that anyone and everyone is amazing.

I guess *everyone*, I realized, would include *me*.

But what was special about me? I wondered. I guess you can't always know what those things are about yourself. Maybe because you're too close to see it, like a flower that looks down and thinks it is just a stem. I guess the important thing is to trust that you are. You're special. And the people close to you see it in more ways than you could ever, ever know.

Before I realized it, my feet had led me to the playhouse where I had been several times in the past for meetings of Imaginaries Anonymous. I wondered if anyone would recognize me. I'd never gotten around to asking what I looked like now. I'd been so busy helping Bernard that I'd forgotten all about it.

"Hello?" I said quietly, creaking open the pink plastic door. "Is this still Imaginaries Anonymous . . ."

"I'm only as invisible as I feel, imaginary or not."

After the group chant, I took a seat in the back and listened to the first speaker, even though I couldn't actually see anyone at the front of the room. The speaker must have been extremely short, I thought. Must have accidentally included the term *elfin* or *Lilliputian* on the reassignment form, poor fool.

"I mean, sure, it was hard at first," said the wee imaginary. "But then I realized, maybe one day I'll float around the entire world. Maybe I'll waft down the Amazon, drift up the Eiffel Tower, get stuck to a fuzzy monkey and live in the top of the highest tree. All in all, I'm one lucky buckaroo."

The other members clapped, and thanked the imaginary for sharing. I felt thankful too, but for another reason. After everyone else shared, and after the cookies and juice, I found my way over to the tiny imaginary.

"*Cowgirl?*" I asked. "Cowgirl, is that really you?"

Chapter Fifty-four
THE WORLD ON A PIECE OF FUZZ

"You're . . . you're . . ." I stammered to Cowgirl, trying to find the word.

"A tiny piece of fuzz," she said, helping me finish the thought.

"Well, yeah," I said. "I mean, what are you? A dandelion seed? Lint? Who would imagine such a thing?"

"His name is Marcel. He's six. He read a book about an elephant that discovered a whole tiny city on a piece of fuzz. Decided he wanted a fuzz of his own, and that's how he got me."

"Makes me wonder," I said, "what you put on *your* form."

"Actually," replied Cowgirl. "I didn't fill mine out. I figured, hey, wherever the wind takes me is fine."

A breeze blew through the playhouse and Cowgirl fluttered around for a few moments before settling back down.

"Literally," I said, and we both laughed. "You know," I added, "I'm still amazed I recognized you."

"Hey," she said. "I recognized you when you were a hot-dog-shaped mutt, didn't I? It's not so hard. You just have to look past the outside. Have you ever noticed that real people are the same way? One of them could age about seventy years, and you'd still recognize them. The secret is in the eyes."

I tried to imagine Bernard's bespectacled eyes, and Merla's full of energy. Not so hard. When I tried to picture Fleur's eyes, the memory was a bit foggier, but Cowgirl was right—there they were, coming into focus after a moment: the color inside like a pond, with blue, and green, and shafts of golden sunlight; a place where you'd still expect a fish to break the surface and leap out at any moment.

"Before you go," said Cowgirl. "I have something of yours."

"Of mine?" I asked. "But I don't own anything. You lose anything you're carrying when you become a new kid's friend."

Cowgirl floated over to the table and hovered

near a napkin. I followed, picked up the napkin, and caught my breath when I saw what was underneath.

"I made a trade for it," she said.

There, on the table, was the compass Fleur had given me, the one I thought I'd lost forever to the Oogly Boogly. It was rare, I knew now, for something you'd let go because you didn't realize its value to then find its way back home to you. I clutched the compass, understanding its real magic— the magic to remind me of what I had lost, and to tell me to appreciate right now, because that too might soon be gone.

Chapter Fifty-five
HOLY FUTURE FAILURE

"Bernard," I said the next day after breakfast. "I've decided we're entering the talent show at school."

Bernard just stared unblinkingly at his cereal spoon like it held a mini-apocalypse.

"Did you hear me?" I asked.

"No," replied Bernard.

"I SAID WE'RE ENTERING THE TALENT SHOW," I shouted.

"I *heard* you," said Bernard, covering his ears. "I meant, no, there's no way I'm entering. Just look at me!"

"You look great," I replied. "Is that a new shirt? Striped is your color, my friend."

"No," said Bernard. "I mean I have no talents. Not a single one. I trip sometimes when I'm just walking. I almost died jumping rope once. I'm allergic to butterflies."

"I don't think any of those problems are a lack of talent," I replied, adding, "Really? Butterflies? Never mind," I said, waving my hand. "Focus. Do you perhaps play an instrument?"

"My cousin once taught me to make armpit whoopee cushion sounds. Here, listen . . ."

"No, it's okay, I believe you," I said. "Sounds like a real bonding experience. Can you juggle? Spin plates? Twirl a flaming baton?"

"No, no, and haven't yet tried but am willing," replied Bernard.

This was turning out to be harder than I'd imagined. We both slumped down on the front steps in defeat. As we did, I heard a clanking in my pocket, and reached in to find the compass that had been returned to me by the cowgirl.

"What's that?" asked Bernard.

"Oh, this allegedly magic compass. I got it at a show with Maurice the Magnificent. He wasn't *that* magnificent, actually, but a little funny, I guess, for an old guy."

And then, as I said the words, my brain-bulb finally lit up.

"I know what your talent is," I informed Bernard. I rubbed my chin like an evil genius or a coach on a makeover show.

"Yes, yes . . ." I said. "Maaaaarvelous."

"Holy future failure," said Bernard with a gulp.

Chapter Fifty-six
BERNARD THE WONDROUS

It's just like they say: Time flies when you're forcing your best friend to do something against his will. Before I knew it, it was the night of the big school talent show.

"Feeling magical?" I asked Bernard.

We were standing backstage. Bernard was wearing a cape and magician's hat. I was wearing a pair of sequined pants and a vest. I thought we looked great, except Bernard had turned a sickly shade of green and it was starting to clash with my sparkles.

"Don't be nervous," I said. "It's just a room full of people, and some judges, and oh! Look who's on next! It's Zoë-of-the-eye-patch. I forgot she was performing too."

Bernard's face went from green to gray. We watched as Zoë performed with her group of friends, and continued

watching as they got in a fight halfway through and had to be pulled off the stage. After that came a metal band, a poet, and three more groups of dancing girls who also got into fights onstage.

"I'm liking these odds," I whispered to Bernard. "Ooh, looks like we're next."

"And now," said the announcer reading off his note card, "the magic of Bernard the Wondrous and his handsome assistant!"

Everyone, including Bernard's dad in the front row and Zoë in the wings, clapped as we wheeled a cabinet out onto the stage.

"For my first trick," said Bernard in a whisper, "I will make my assistant disappear."

"What?" shouted someone from the back of the auditorium. "Speak up, kid, can't hear you!"

"I said," said Bernard more audibly, "I will now make my assistant disappear!"

I elbowed Bernard.

"My *handsome* assistant," he corrected.

Whispers and mumbles went through the crowd.

What assistant?

Do you see someone?

Is this kid crazy?

I stepped inside the cabinet with my usual flair and grace. Bernard closed the door. Then, with a dramatic, albeit awkward, flourish, he pranced around, waved his arms, and shouted out several rounds of "Alakazam!" and "Abracadabra!" and "Shazam!" After that, he opened the door to reveal . . .

An empty cabinet!

"Ta-da," said Bernard.

Well, I have to tell you, it was so silent in that auditorium that you could have heard a baby mouse hiccup or a flea scratch an itch. I'd never seen so many people with their mouths hanging open and their foreheads scrunched up in confusion.

But then—Huzzah!—from somewhere in the back of the room I heard a giggle. Actually, more of a guffaw. And this, it seemed, was contagious, because before we knew it, laughter was coming from every part of the room, louder and louder, like perfect, twinkling music.

They clapped again for Bernard's next trick, where he sawed his invisible assistant in half.

They chuckled when he made invisible me levitate. They hooted as he passed my body through a silver hoop. And they simply howled when Bernard stuck a sword through my imaginary head.

A comedic genius! they shouted.

Funniest act by far!

Bernard the Wondrous for the win!

Chapter Fifty-seven
AND HIS LOVELY ASSISTANT

After the show I watched as Bernard was greeted by several
of his classmates, some of whom I was fairly certain hadn't
known his name until that night.

You should be a professional comedian, they said.

How'd you ever come up with something so good? they asked.

Maybe you should sit with us at lunch.

And it just got better from there.

On Monday Bernard got picked fourth-from-last for playground kickball. Fourth-from-last! Usually he wasn't picked
at all, so this was a huge improvement. And during the game
he didn't have to hide in the bushes or enlist the help of any
foliage at all.

On Tuesday Bernard put his hand up for the first time all
year, and gave the answer to the capital of Idaho. At lunch he

didn't sit alone, and when the bus reached Bernard's house, he was totally noticeable enough that the driver didn't forget his stop.

On Wednesday Zoë, who looked even nicer with both eyes, asked Bernard if he was going to the school dance. Bernard said he'd probably stop by, and Zoë said—wait for it—*see you there*. See you there! In the fourth grade, that basically means they were engaged.

On Thursday the principal presented Bernard with his talent show trophy: first place, and it even had *Bernard the Wondrous* etched on a little gold plate on the front. Beneath that were the four most amazing words of all: *and His Lovely Assistant*. Holy fame! Holy fortune!

Everything was great.

So great, in fact, that by Friday I realized the sad truth: It was time for me to go.

The invisible boy was no longer invisible. He wouldn't be able to just float around anymore. Or hide during games. Or not join in. Because now he had been seen.

So I went.

I didn't have the heart to say good-bye.

I knew he'd ask me to stay, and if he did, I would. Bernard

was like a turtle that had just started to poke his head outside his own shell. If I stuck around, he'd retreat back inside to the safety of my company at the slightest spook. And I didn't want Bernard to go back into hiding, that was for sure. I wanted to hold on to this feeling of pride that I had truly helped change someone's life. And that, I thought, made me just a little less invisible. Yes, I'd go back to the reassignment office to explain it all, and they'd give me a new home.

As I watched Bernard polishing his trophy and laughing with new friends, I realized he'd done many tricks and done them well, but there was one that made him truly great: Bernard the Wondrous had, finally, made himself appear.

Chapter Fifty-eight
EIGHT HUNDRED BILLION NEW STARS

So I left, toward what I didn't know. A new assignment, I supposed. A new spot on the Map of Me.

Bernard, I thought, had a map as well. His was one of those really special maps. You know the kind where when you look at it, it just looks like a blank sheet of parchment, but with the right super-secret decoder glasses, you can see everything little by little. The mermaid lagoons, the magician's mountain, and yes, the colors—all the colors that they don't even have words for yet, there on the Map of Bernard.

With nowhere else to go, I made my way to the Office of Reassignment. I told them I didn't need to fill out a form. I answered no questions. I even crumpled up the sheet for dramatic effect, thinking *just send me wherever I'm needed most.* I waited in the empty waiting room, and when my number was called, I went through the small door to meet my new life, ready for whatever might come.

But I had forgotten what had happened at the very start of my journey: If you don't fill out a form, you are sent into the limbo. The dark. To wait. For what could be a very, very long time.

And that's exactly where I found myself.

I decided to pretend I was just playing hide-and-seek. I reminded myself that lots of things were happening outside the dark. I imagined them all.

One billion and sixty-four million babies have been born while you've been hiding in this toy chest, I would think. *Also, eight thousand five hundred and eighty-six species went extinct; four hundred and eighty volcanoes erupted; twelve hundred people died from coconuts falling on their heads; four hundred sixteen Mondays passed, and Tuesdays, Wednesdays, Thursdays, and Fridays; the moon orbited the earth one hundred and four times; eight hundred billion new stars were born in the galaxy.*

But for me there were no new stars. There was only dark. And the dark was beginning to take me away.

Everything was beginning to fade.

It was like my memories were sculpted out of sand and then carelessly left too near the water. They were becoming ethereal, intangible, invisible. And I didn't know what to do to make them stay.

First, I watched my name leave.

The *J* floated away like a fat bubble, followed by the *A, C, Q, U, E,* and *S* all taken in one swoop. The *P-A-P-I-E-R* took a tad longer, first the ink blurring and the letters finally falling apart into floating snippets—the moon-curve of a *P,* and the fork tongs of an *E* getting caught on each other, then finally fading in an origami letter tango. I let go of the maps I'd drawn, my favorite songs, and every person whom I'd met and known and cared for. Good-bye, Fleur's kindness, my mother's patience, and my father's sense of wonder; good-bye, Pierre's creativity, Merla's huge heart, and Bernard's bravery; farewell to Cowgirl's sense of adventure, to Stinky Sock, Mr. Pitiful, and all the other imaginaries; good-bye to the way they cared more about the happiness of their friends than about their own. All those memories flipped fins and swam away like a school of impossible, invisible, imaginary flying fish.

And then, I was really, truly alone.

Who are you when everything you've ever known about yourself is gone?

Who are you when there's nobody around to remind you of your role, and no memories to regret or keep you warm?

What would you look like if you couldn't remember ever looking like anything? What form would you take?

What would you dream at night if you had no memories? What notes would get stuck in your head if you remembered no songs?

After everything had faded, there in the dark, I tried to see myself. I was no shape in particular, of course, but that's okay. I'd learned that didn't mean a thing. So what was I? My memories may have faded, but the people I'd known were a part of me. They had *made* me. And in that way, I realized, just by being myself, I am with them—with all their kindness and bravery and selflessness. I didn't need any map or compass to find it, this place they had helped to build. And so I filled the home inside myself with furniture; with laughter and light, with love and a family. I imagined I could soar there through a sky full of Autumn Mist, and when I arrived, I would know I was home, finally, after so much time spent far, far away.

Chapter Fifty-nine
GILLS AND WINGS AND
SCALES OF GREEN

So much time had passed that when the dark limbo finally ended, I wasn't quite sure what I was seeing. Had I experienced light before? Or had I only imagined it?

I was in a child's room. It looked like a dream, like a combination of all the bedrooms I had known before. The boards creaked. Somewhere in the distance I heard a dog barking. The air smelled like fresh laundry, and pine, and the hint of finally being free.

The window was open, and the curtains blew around and danced. It sounds foolish, but I felt like crying then, just a tiny bit. Had windows dancing in the wind always been so beautiful? Had creaking floors, and barking dogs, and dancing dust in shafts of slanted light? I suppose it takes being locked away from *everything* to finally really appreciate *anything*.

Where was I? *What* was I? I climbed out the window, and once on the grass I looked at my legs. They were covered in scales of vivid, bright, emerald green. I touched my neck and felt gills. I moved my back and realized, to my shock, that I had *wings*.

I flexed my muscles and the wings moved.

"I wonder . . ." I said, and pushed my feet off the ground. And wouldn't you know it: It appeared I knew how to fly. Had I always known? It seemed too extraordinary to be something I had done before and forgotten.

I got the hang of it rather quickly, and went up higher and higher into the sky.

As I flew, I watched golden-yellow fields dotted with cows below, and rolling green hills with no houses, no fences. I saw the green give way to sand, and dunes, and then across the water more houses and more roads. I didn't know where I was going—it seemed I had some sort of inner compass, so I followed it, flying on into the evening.

Finally, I had the sensation, somehow, that I had arrived.

I could see a street below. Like many things in life, it too went around in a circle. I landed softly, though a bit loudly, in the quiet neighborhood. The street sign said Cherry Lane, the sun had just set, and all the children were being called inside from their playing for the night.

I felt as if my mind had been a black-and-white drawing, and somehow everything was starting to fill in with color. I looked at the yellow house in front of me, the red mailbox, the purple flowers. A square of warmth formed around the porch light. It looked like an invitation, like the last outpost in a huge world.

Someone, I thought, *left that porch light on for me.*

Chapter Sixty
WELCOME HOME, JACQUES PAPIER

I walked up the steps to the house with the warm light. There was something familiar about the peeling paint on the porch, and I stopped cold when I saw two letters, a *J* and an *F*, carved in the side of a tree.

I've been here before, I thought. *A long, long time ago.*

I was about to push open the screen door when I heard a snarl at my feet. I looked down, and there was the oldest dog I had ever seen. His body was long, his legs short, and his belly dragged on the ground. His fur was gray and patchy, and his eyes were clouded over with age. Even though he growled in a distinctly inhospitable way, I had the odd feeling we were very old friends.

Or, at the least, very old enemies.

"Don't mind him."

I looked up, and standing on the other side of the door was a little girl of about seven, maybe eight. She had red hair, and when she smiled she did so with a twinkle in her eyes.

"I'm Felice," said the girl. "I'd invite you in, but I really don't think you'll fit."

So instead, she led me to the back of the house and gave me a cup of what she said was a cloud root beer float and a plate of moon grilled cheeses. I looked around as I ate. *I've played here before*, I thought again—I've jumped in leaves in this yard, and drawn maps, and made up endless games. But when? With whom?

The back door opened, and out stepped a girl in her teens, with the same red hair as Felice.

"You were right," whispered Felice to the older girl. "I imagined a friend, and he actually *came*. I think he *flew* here."

"Ah," said the girl, standing with her arm around her sister. "A flying friend. That's special. What does he look like?"

"Can't you see him?" asked Felice. "He's right there. He's giant!"

"No," said the older girl. "People my age don't have imaginary friends."

"Well, he seems to be part dragon and part fish," explained

166

Felice. "And he eats cloud root beer floats and moon grilled cheeses, but his favorite food is stardust."

"Oh!" said the older girl. Her face looked surprised, but she smiled again after a moment. "I know what he is," she continued. "He's a Dragon Herring."

Felice considered this, and then nodded, deciding her big sister was, as usual, absolutely right.

"He'll need a name," said Felice.

"I believe he already has one," said her sister.

And though she had said she could not see me, the older girl came closer and looked—I could swear—right into my eyes.

And that's when I realized there was something familiar in this girl's eyes. The color inside was like a pond, with blue, and green, and shafts of golden sunlight. Why, I expected a fish to break the surface and leap out at any moment.

I knew those eyes. Something inside me broke, and split open. I don't know how, but when I lowered my head, the girl who could not see me leaned against my invisible emerald-green scales and closed her eyes. And there, for one brief moment, we were just a little boy and a little girl. They made up endless maps together—he would be captain of the forest and she would be navigator. In the glowing late summer light, they carved two initials, one *J* and one *F*, into the side of the tree. They gathered magic in their small hands, tumbled home each evening, and fell asleep with leaves of grass in their hair.

So much love stirred in my heart, I thought it would burst. And though I knew she could not hear me, though I knew my words would be lost, I wanted to tell her anyhow.

"*Fleur*," I whispered. "*I didn't forget you.*

"*Fleur*," I said. "*I came back.*"

Then: "*Welcome home*," she said. "*Welcome home, Jacques Papier.*"

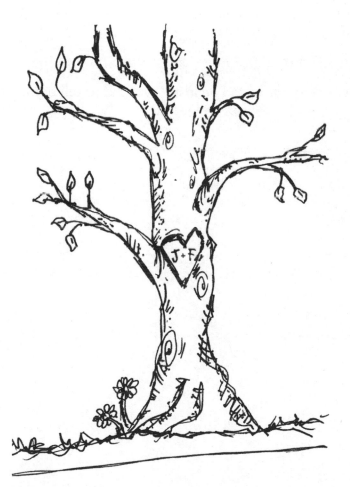

Acknowledgments

For helping on this journey to tell my story, I would like to thank Fleur and Felice Papier, my mom and dad, Maurice the Magnificent, Cowgirl, Mr. Pitiful, Stinky Sock, The Everything, The Office of Reassignment, Pierre, Merla, and Bernard.

Last (and least), I would like to thank François the Evil Wiener Dog: Every great tale needs a low-down, dirty villain, and nobody is closer to the ground than you.

~Jacques Papier, Memoirist

I am grateful to Emily Van Beek for being someone I trust and admire more than words; Nancy Conescu, editor extraordinaire, this ending is as much yours as mine; Lauri Hornik, for her reflection, guidance, and for saying Yes! when I (nervously) asked to illustrate; Sarah Wartell, Josh Ludmir, Jake Currie, and Patrick O'Donnell for their enthusiasm of said silly drawings; and finally, to my family and friends, in the words of Jacques Papier:

"Everyone feels invisible sometimes . . ."

True. But you all make me feel infinitely less so.

~Michelle Cuevas, Author